I0451687

A Banging New Year

Hot Holidays Book 2

Ellis O. Day

Copyright © 2020 Ellis O. Day

All rights reserved.

978-1-942706-82-3

All rights reserved. This book or any portion thereof may not be reproduced or used in any manner whatsoever without the express written permission of the publisher except for the use of brief quotations in a book review.

This is a work of fiction. Names, characters, businesses, places, events and incidents are either the products of the author's imagination or used in a fictitious manner. Any resemblance to actual persons, living or dead, or actual events is purely coincidental.

I love to hear from readers so email me at
authorEllisOday@gmail.com

https://www.EllisODay.com

Follow me

Facebook
https://www.facebook.com/EllisODayRomanceAuthor/

Closed FB Group (sneak peeks, sample chapters, and other bonuses)
https://www.facebook.com/groups/153238782143373

Bookbub
https://www.bookbub.com/authors/Ellis-o-day

Instagram
https://www.instagram.com/authorEllisOday/

Twitter
https://twitter.com/Ellis_o_day

Join My Readers' Group and for a limited time get the entire Six Nights of Sin series for FREE

(THERE'S A PEEK OF BOOK ONE AT THE END OF THIS BOOK)

Join my newsletter to get your FREE books

CHAPTER 1: ADRIAN

Adrian stood by the bar at The Blue Newb watching the sea of well-dressed, young adults grind and sway to the music. He grabbed his sister's arm as she headed toward the dance floor with a guy.

"Stop it." Paige slapped his hand. "I'm not doing anything but going to dance."

He let go of her. She was a lost cause. All his sisters were. He stepped in front of the guy. "I'm her big brother and a Marine. You grind on her and I'll bust your jaw and feed your nuts to the squirrels."

"Adrian." Paige slugged his shoulder. "Go away." She took her dance partner's hand, dragging him to the floor but the guy wasn't nearly as eager as he had been.

"Well played." Colin leaned against the bar, sipping a beer. "I should've thought of that with Anne Marie." He nodded at his youngest sister who was dancing way to close to some stranger.

"Never go through your sister. They'll ignore you or do the opposite to spite you, but the guys...They'll fear you. They know what they want to do and most of them have their own sisters." He scanned the crowded club for Ellie for the hundredth time. He was starting to lose hope. Fate could be a lying bitch sometimes.

"You're a smart man."

"I had to learn at a young age how to maneuver

through a household full of women. You're lucky. You only have two sisters."

"Two is more than enough." Colin shivered. "I can't even imagine having six. You deserve a medal."

"Yeah, I do." He laughed.

Colin was a good guy. They'd spent the last hour or so watching over their sisters and their sisters' friends and helping each other out when one of the friends got too grabby with them. Neither of them had said anything but they seemed to agree that nineteen to twenty-one-year-old females were too young for them.

His gaze stopped on a curvy brunette and then moved along. Her hair was too dark and too straight.

"Not here yet, huh?"

"What are you talking about?" Damn, he'd been caught.

"Whatever woman you're waiting for."

"I'm not."

Colin gave him a look that made it clear he wasn't buying that lie.

"Fine. No, she's not here."

"Stood up. That sucks."

"It does but that's not what happened."

"Right." Colin laughed. "Keep telling yourself that."

"It's more like I'm a surprise. She has no idea I'm going to be here."

"Is she going to be happy about this surprise?"

"She'll pretend she's not, but she will be." Their Christmas Eve sexcapades had been way too good for her not to want a repeat performance. He sure as fuck did.

Colin snorted. "Lies we tell ourselves, man."

Adrian's eyes landed on Ellie. She was at a table in the corner sitting with another woman and a man. The guy was older, with dark hair and a serious demeanor.

The man leaned over and said something to Ellie, and she smiled. Jealousy flared in Adrian's gut. He was glad she was having a good time, but he didn't want her to be having too much fun until he joined them. He was her good time guy, no one else.

"Which one?" asked Colin.

"The one in blue."

Ellie wore a royal blue dress that seemed to sparkle with the lights. It was low cut, displaying the tops of her fabulous tits but trapping the rest beneath the fabric. He couldn't wait to set them free and play with them.

Paige strode up to him. "You. Stop being such an ass."

"What did I do?" He forced his gaze away from Ellie.

"You're scaring away every guy I like."

"That's why I'm here."

"It is not."

"Want me to call Mom and Dad and ask?" He pulled his phone from his pocket.

"Mom will side with me. We were just going to dance. That's it."

"Really?" He pressed the record button and videotaped some of the dancers grinding against each other. He turned the phone toward her and pressed play. "You think Mom will be okay with you dancing like this?"

"You are the worst brother ever."

"Then I'm doing my job."

"Arghh." Paige stormed away to join her friends.

His eyes went back to Ellie. It wasn't going to be easy to woo her and to watch his sister, but he was a former Marine. He could do it.

"Do you have a shot?" asked Colin.

"A shot at what?"

"With her. This woman you've been waiting for."

"Oh yeah. Better than a shot."

"You sure? She seems into that other guy."

"She isn't." At least, she'd better not be. "She wants me."

"Hmm."

"Her body does. I'm positive about that and I can worry about her mind later."

"That's good enough for me. Go. I've got the girls."

"What?" He pulled his eyes away from Ellie.

"One of us should have a good New Year's Eve."

"I don't know." He was responsible for Paige.

"Seriously, I'll keep her safe. She's around my parents' house so much she's like my sister."

"But she's not." He looked at the guy closer.

"I'm not into little girls and she and my sister are children in my eyes."

"Don't fuck with me on this. I'm not twelve anymore." Now, he was big enough to kill the fucker if anything happened to Paige, unlike when Colin broke his oldest sister's heart in high school.

4

"I won't. Plus, you're right over there. You can still watch out for her. I'll just take over threatening the frat boys while you focus on something else."

Colin was right. He could flirt with Ellie and watch his sister.

CHAPTER 2: ELLIE

Ellie leaned over by Alison as Harker walked away with the manager of The Blue Newb.

"He likes you." She poked Alison's arm.

"Who? The manager? You think?" Alison stared at the two men.

"No, not the manager. Harker."

"Barker? No." Alison chuckled. "I drive him crazy. He's said it a hundred times."

"I thought his name was Harker?" She was so embarrassed. She'd been calling the man the wrong name all night.

"It is but I call him Barker in my head because all he does is bark at me." She lowered her voice, imitating Harker's. "Alison, the program isn't fast enough. Alison, my computer isn't working. What did you do to it? Alison, shut up for one second so I can think." She rolled her eyes. "That man doesn't talk; he yells."

"I didn't notice that. All I see is a guy who can barely take his eyes off you."

"Plllleeeese."

"I'm serious."

"Well, if you're right, it's too bad," said Alison.

"Why? He's hot."

"He's my boss and I'm not desperate enough to hook up with a guy who bitches at me all the time." Alison frowned and took a sip of her drink. "But give me another month of celibacy and I might be."

"Maybe if you were nicer to him."

"Me?" Alison downed her margarita. "I'm a saint." She waved at their waitress, signaling another round and then nudged Ellie's arm. "Drink up. I'm not going to be the only one sloppy drunk tonight."

"I can't. I have to deal with Marc tomorrow. It'll be bad enough without the hangover."

"Why isn't he out of your apartment again?"

"It's not my apartment. He's on the lease too."

"And he won't leave?"

"Nope. He refuses."

"Don't you pay all the bills?" Alison handed the waitress some money as she dropped off the two drinks.

"I do." One more thing in her life that was unfair.

"Then stop."

"I can't. It'll screw up my credit."

"What are you going to do? You can't keep living with the cheating jerk."

"I'm not sleeping with him if that's what you think. I've been crashing on the couch because the asshole won't give up the bed but not for too much longer. The lease is up in a couple of weeks. Then I'll sign without him and he'll have to leave."

Alison pushed Ellie's glass toward her. "Drink up. I don't think you're going to have to worry about dealing with Marc tonight or tomorrow."

"Why do you—"

"Look who's here and he's even better looking than his picture." Alison grabbed her head and turned it toward the dance floor. "I wonder if he's watched any porn." She squeezed Ellie's arm. "If not, you could take him home and teach him a thing or two. You're so lucky."

"Oh shit." Ellie grabbed her drink and gulped it down. Suddenly, getting drunk was probably the only way she was going to make it through the night without having her head explode.

CHAPTER 3: ADRIAN

Adrian made his way across the club, his eyes never leaving Ellie. She looked gorgeous. Her hair was pulled up in some sort of messy bun that his fingers itched to undo. He wanted to watch those silky, soft tresses tumble down over her breasts—preferably, her naked breasts.

He knew the moment she saw him. Not only because the other woman forced Ellie's head his way, but because her eyes widened in surprise before she chugged her drink. Normally, he wouldn't take that as a good sign, but her eyes had also taken a quick trip down his body. She wanted him even though she'd pretend she didn't.

"Ellie." He stopped at the table and then turned his attention to the other woman. "Alison?" They'd never met but this had to be Ellie's friend who he'd spoken with on Christmas during the car ride to Ellie's parents' house.

"Adrian." Alison pushed out the chair between her and Ellie. "It's so great to actually meet you in person. Join us."

"I'm sure he's busy," said Ellie.

"Not at all." He started to sit.

"That's Harker's chair." Ellie grabbed it, trying to push

it back by the table but Alison clung to the other side.

"Harker's not here," said Alison.

Adrian stepped back as the two played tug-o-war with the chair for a second before it slid toward Alison and almost knocked her off her seat.

"Sit." Alison shoved it toward him.

Ellie glared at her friend, but Adrian ignored her, sitting and sliding the chair a little closer to Ellie as he scooted it up by the table.

"May I buy you ladies a drink?" Their glasses were full, but it was always polite to offer.

"I'm good," said Ellie.

"You are that," he muttered.

"Shots," said Alison. "Let's do shots."

"Ah…sure." He waved at the waitress.

"I don't want a shot," said Ellie.

"Too bad. You need one." Alison turned to the waitress. "Bring us three shots of tequila."

"I'm not getting plastered just because you want to," said Ellie.

The waitress hesitated.

"Okay." Alison's eyes gleamed. "We'll play a game."

"What kind of game?" Ellie watched her friend like a rabbit watched a snake.

"You have to drink a shot every time you're mean to Adrian."

"I like this game," he mumbled around his beer.

"I'm not mean to him."

"Ha. Still lying I see." This time he didn't mumble.

"I'm not lying, and I'm not mean to you." Ellie elbowed him in the arm.

"You are too," said Alison.

"And you're mean to Harker."

"She is that." The man who'd been at the table with the two women earlier pulled out a chair on the other side of Alison and sat.

"I'm not mean to you. Sticking up for myself is not the same as what she does." Alison sent Ellie a smug look.

Adrian looked at Harker. The man was as amused as he was, and the other guy was definitely interested in Alison so tonight was perfect. "I'm Adrian and she's very mean to me." He held out his hand and the other man shook it.

"Harker."

"How many shots?" asked the waitress, growing impatient.

"Bring a shot glass, a bottle of Jose 1800, limes and salt." Harker handed her his credit card.

"We don't sell by the bottle."

"You do to me." Harker pointed over her shoulder where a dark-haired guy in a suit was talking to a table of women. "Verify it with your manager."

"Okay." The waitress left.

"Now, let's establish the rules for this game," said Harker.

"Ellie drinks every time she's mean to Adrian," said Alison.

"And Alison drinks whenever she's mean to you," said

Ellie.

"I'm not…"

Harker touched Alison's lips. "Shut up for one second, okay?"

Adrian winced. His sisters would've bitten off the man's finger and torn out his eyes for that, but Alison just bristled, slapping Harker's hand away.

"I'll presume there'll be some contention over what's classified as mean so we'll vote." Harker's eyes met Adrian's with a clear message. If they worked together, they'd always win because the women were working against each other.

"Sounds good to me." He tipped his head slightly, letting the other man know that he understood.

"And when do you two drink?" asked Ellie.

"When we're mean to the two of you." It seemed simple to him and perfect because he had no intention of being mean to Ellie.

"That's not fair. You're never mean to me because you want to get me back into your…." Ellie stopped, her face heating.

"No reason to hide it. I think we all know what's on the table." Harker's dark gaze drifted to Alison, but she didn't even notice.

The waitress came back and put the shot glass, limes, salt and full bottle of tequila on the table. She handed Harker his credit card.

"Keep our other drinks full too." Harker gave her a couple of bills and at least one of them was a hundred.

"Yes, sir." She strolled away.

Alison opened the tequila, poured it into the glass and slid it to Ellie. "Drink. You were mean to Adrian."

"I was not."

"You were," he whispered none too quietly.

"When?"

"As soon as I walked over to your table."

"I wasn't mean." Ellie glanced at Harker. "I didn't want Alison to give away your seat." She smiled softly and Adrian was pretty sure she was batted her eyelashes. "So, it was actually Alison who was mean to you." She slid the shot across the table to her frenemy.

Adrian wasn't letting her get out of this so easily. "She didn't even say hi. I hadn't seen her since I drove her all the way to her parents' house on Christmas and she couldn't even say hi to me."

"Is that true?" asked Harker.

Ellie's mouth opened and then shut. Even she knew she'd lost this one, but she wasn't going down without a fight. "Yes, but only because I didn't want him to take your seat."

"That wasn't mean," said Harker.

Ellie smiled but Adrian sent the guy a look that said – what the fuck? They were supposed to be on the same team.

"It was rude." Harker pushed the glass toward Ellie and picked up the bottle. "And that's two drinks."

"Still want to save his seat?" Alison burst out laughing.

"Okay, but he"—Ellie pointed at Adrian—"drinks

whenever he's cocky."

"Now, wait one moment." That was a dangerous rule. He was always cocky.

"That's the only way I'm playing." Elle gave him a challenging look.

"Don't be a pussy," said Harker. "You can't be that arrogant."

Adrian shrugged. "Obviously, you don't know me very well, but I'll play. I like tequila."

CHAPTER 4: ELLIE

"Look at him." Ellie slapped Alison's arm. She was so irritated with Adrian. He'd sat here for hours, playing the drinking game with them and now he was flirting his way across the club. Okay, he was just walking back from the bathroom, but he may as well be flirting as he squeezed through the crowd with a sexy smile on his face.

"Look at what?" Alison stared in the direction Ellie was looking.

"Adrian, and that counts. He has to drink." It was only fair. The man had no right to have an ass that every freaking woman in the bar noticed.

"What are you talking about?" asked Harker.

"Please. He's being arrogant." She looked at Alison for help. "Explain it to him." She lifted her glass and sucked the last of the alcohol from the ice. "I thought you told that waitress to keep our drinks full?"

"I did." Harker gave her a condescending look. "Until the two of you took it too far."

"Too far," she and Alison screeched at the same time. She glanced at her friend and they both started

15

laughing. Tonight was turning out to be a lot of fun, except for these two guys.

"Exactly." Harker's tone was dry and humorless. "Neither of you can handle your alcohol."

"I can handle it just fine." She waved her glass at the waitress.

"What can you handle?" Adrian sat.

Ellie was almost positive that he was closer to her than he had been before he went to the bathroom. There's no way she'd missed the soft press of his leg against hers. It made her want to trail her fingernails up his thigh and over that lovely dick of his. The damn man was driving her nuts—smelling good, making her laugh and being heart-stoppingly hot when he smiled at her.

She picked up the bottle of tequila and leaned closer to him, sloshing that beautiful, gold liquid-magic into the shot glass. She wanted the other women to know that he was hers even though he wasn't. Men like him never belonged to a woman for long. They always cheated but…Oh, it was so lovely when all that alpha masculine focus was on her. Right now, she had his attention. She was drunk. He was sexy as sin and she was horny. She hadn't had sex since…that night with him. Her libido went into overdrive. She put the glass in front of him. "You, my friend, have to drink."

"Why do I have to drink? I didn't do anything arrogant."

"You did too." She slapped his arm. "You always do. Now, drink."

16

"No." He pushed the glass aside. "I'm not drinking until you tell me what I did."

"Please, you know what you did." Everything he did screamed arrogance and self-assurance.

"Help me out here," he turned to Harker.

"I have no idea." Harker frowned at both women with a sort of slightly amused disgust. "They're wasted."

"Yeah, they are," said Adrian.

"We are not." Alison grabbed Ellie's hand. "She's right about Adrian." She poked Harker's shoulder. "And you know it. You just don't want to admit I'm right."

"What exactly did Adrian do that was arrogant? Hell, he wasn't even at the table," said Harker.

"He..." Alison paused, turning toward Ellie. "He...What did he do?"

"He walked." Ellie pushed the drink back toward him, crossing her arms over her chest.

"Arrogantly?" asked Harker before turning to Adrian. "How does one do that?"

"I couldn't tell you." Adrian laughed but his eyes were on that girl. That young girl he'd been watching all night.

She was thin and pretty and looked like a teenager. It wouldn't be long before Adrian excused himself and went to that girl's side, forgetting Ellie completely.

"You're such an ass." She was done. She wasn't going to sit here and be humiliated again. Her ex, Marc, had done enough of that on Christmas Eve. She pulled her phone from her purse.

"What are you doing?" Adrian grabbed her wrist.

"I'm going home." She yanked her hand from his.

"Why? It's not midnight yet."

"What do you care. It's not like I'm going to kiss you."

"That's mean," said Adrian. "She drinks, not me."

"I don't care." Right now, she wanted to go home and sleep. Her choice in men was getting worse. At least Marc had remained faithful while he was chasing her.

"What's wrong with her?" asked Harker.

"I haven't a clue." Adrian watched her like he would a bomb that was about to explode.

"Oh please, don't act like you don't know." She scanned through her phone, looking for that damn Uber app but her fingers weren't working too well.

"I'm not acting. I truly have no idea why you're so pissed."

"Do you think I didn't see. I have eyes." She pointed at her face.

"I see that." He seemed to be trying not to laugh but the bastard should try harder because this wasn't funny.

She turned and pointed. "Her."

"What about her?" But he was no longer amused.

"I see you don't like being caught. You guys never do."

"Being caught doing what?" He seemed actually confused but she wasn't falling for it.

"Don't even try to tell me that you haven't been checking her out all night." She pointed again at the young woman, hating her and then hating herself for blaming the girl. It wasn't the other woman's fault that Adrian was a two-faced asshole.

"You have been watching her," said Harker.

"I have." Adrian grinned as he turned back toward Ellie. "And you're jealous."

"I'm not jealous. I just think it's rude." Her eyes went to Harker's. "He has to drink twice for that."

CHAPTER 5: ADRIAN

Oh, this was perfect. Ellie was jealous and that meant she wanted him. Adrian was going to use this to make sure she was back in his bed tonight. Unfortunately, that meant he had to drink. He grimaced as he stared at the shot. He'd had more than enough alcohol. Ellie had been brutal. She'd caught every smart-assed thing he'd said and labeled it as arrogant. Harker had tried to side with him as often as he could, but Adrian was an admittedly cocky guy.

"Drink." Ellie pushed the shot glass closer to his hand, almost spilling it before picking up the bottle. "Hurry up, you've gotta drink twice for being rude." The bottle swayed with her arm.

"Okay."

Ellie smiled. It was wide and honest, lighting up her face but all his drunk, horny mind could see was her opening those lips and sliding her pink tongue up his cock.

He forced that thought aside. First, get her to go home with him. Second, get her to suck his dick. "On one condition."

"Figures, he'd have a condition," muttered Alison.

"That wasn't nice." He grinned at Harker.

"He's right. It wasn't." Harker took the tequila from Ellie and put it in front of Alison's lips. "Drink."

She opened her mouth and then closed it quickly before he could tip up the bottle. "Wait. I don't have to be nice to him."

"Still sharp even when sloshed." Harker smiled.

Alison smiled back. "Thank you…Hey, I'm not drunk."

"It still wasn't nice," Adrian muttered.

"Sorry," said Alison.

"Don't be sorry. He deserves it," said Ellie.

"That isn't nice." Harker handed the tequila to Ellie. "You drink."

"Fine but he drinks first." She took the bottle.

"Only if you agree to my condition." More than likely they'd end up together. An evening of flirting and drinking stacked the odds in his favor, but there was still a chance she'd refuse him. He couldn't let that happen to his dick. It'd been looking forward to a repeat with Ellie for a week.

"Fine." She said it like he was the most exasperating person on the planet. "What's your condition?"

"If you're wrong you go home with me tonight."

"Oh…" Alison leaned forward. "This is getting good."

"There's no way I'm going home with you, not even on a bet," said Ellie.

"You're afraid to lose because you know you're wrong." He'd play on her competitive personality.

"Wrong about what?"

"Wrong about anything."

"Anything?" Harker butted into the conversation. "That's kind of vague."

"I thought we were on the same side." He didn't need logic. He needed her.

"I don't join a losing team." Harker shrugged. "Try harder next time."

"I told you he was a jerk." Alison shoved Harker's shoulder.

"I see what you mean." Suddenly, he and Alison were on the same team.

"Why thank you, Alison. I think that's the nicest thing you've ever called me," said Harker.

"I've never called you anything bad." Alison lowered her voice a little and leaned closer to Adrian. "Not when he was close enough to hear me."

"You have the voice of a Roman orator," said Harker.

"I don't think that's a compliment." Alison laughed and Harker grinned.

"Uh, oh." Ellie slapped Adrian's arm. "You're in trouble now. Your girlfriend is coming over here."

"My girlfrie…" Shit. Colin, Paige and her friends headed their way. He had to do something fast. He pushed the shot glass toward Ellie. "Drink. You were mean."

"You were rude. You drink twice." She pushed it back, tequila sloshing over the side.

"Agree to my condition"—he lifted the glass—"and I will."

"I can't swear I was right about everything."

"What a surprise coming from the little liar," he

22

muttered.

"I'm not a liar." She made a face at him.

"Okay. How about this?" He had to sell this and he had to do it fast. "If you were wrong about something that you made me drink for, then you come home with me tonight."

"Wrong about you being arrogant? Ha. Fine."

He wanted to shout in triumph. She was his.

She stopped his hand before he tossed back the drink. "On one condition."

"What's that?" His senses heightened like he was on patrol. It was just like life to dangle everything he wanted right in his face before snatching it away.

"Even if I was wrong about something—which I wasn't—I only go home with you if you don't do anything to annoy me for the rest of tonight."

"Don't agree to that," said Harker. "The way you walked annoyed her earlier."

"That's because he's so arrogant," said Ellie.

"I can't help how I walk. And why were you watching me? Were you checking out my ass?" He leaned closer. "I'll let you touch it if you're nice."

"See? See how he is?" Ellie stared at the other two.

"Last chance." His sister and her friends had stopped to chat with some other young women, but they were moving again. "If you want me to drink, agree to go home with me. Unless you're afraid of losing."

"I'm not afraid because I won't lose. I'll take your bet. I go home with you if I made you drink when I shouldn't have, and you don't do anything stupid or annoying." She touched his arm, stopping his protest. "And the other two have to agree that it was stupid or annoying."

He glanced at Harker. He needed to know if he could count on the guy. Harker nodded slightly. "Deal." He held out his hand and she shook it. His night was set as soon as he got rid of Paige. His eyes darted toward his sister.

"I can't believe you're still checking her out." Ellie gave him a disgusted look.

"I'm not checking her out. I swear." He chuckled.

"Now, who's lying?" Ellie's tone was disgusted.

"Not me."

"Just drink." She picked up the bottle of tequila.

He tossed back the shot. She filled it again and he shivered. He didn't want another drink, but his sister was only a few feet away. He downed the shot and dropped the glass on the table. "Done. I drank twice because you said I was rude."

"You were."

"Was I?" He stood. "Is it rude to watch out for your baby sister in a club like this?"

"Your sister?" Ellie turned as Paige and her friends moved closer. She glanced at Alison and Harker. "His sister?"

Alison shrugged.

"Salut." Harker raised his glass, a half-smile on his face.

"Adrian," Paige ran up to him. "I'm ready to leave but this dork"—she pointed at Colin—"won't let me until I clear it with you."

"Where are you going?"

"There's a party on campus. Mom doesn't need you chaperoning me for a party on campus "

"That's right. She doesn't"—his gaze met Ellie's and even he'd admit he probably looked pretty damn cocky right now—"which means I have the entire night free."

Harker laughed and Ellie looked like she was going to puke.

CHAPTER 6: ELLIE

"I wasn't wrong," Ellie said as soon as Adrian sat back down after saying goodbye to his sister and her friends.

"Oh, you were so wrong." He leaned back on his chair, his hands behind his head. "Did you want to stay here until midnight or leave now and ring in the new year together."

"More like bang in the new year," muttered Alison.

Harker laughed not even flinching at Ellie's glare.

"That's not going to happen, I wasn't wrong." She tilted up her chin, doing her best to maintain her composure but it wasn't easy. Her body screamed hurrah while her brain…No, it couldn't be her brain. That organ had quit functioning a few shots ago or she'd never have agreed to Adrian's bet. It had to be her instincts sending up warning flags like it was a parade.

"You are such a little liar." Adrian leaned close, his lips almost touching hers. "You're cute but I'll need to punish you for all these lies. I have to keep your moral character in mind."

"My moral…" She pushed him away not even wanting to think about why the idea of this man punishing her was making her wet. "I'm not lying." She was sticking with that. "I said you were checking her out and you were."

"She's my sister. I was not checking her out." He shivered. "That's disgusting."

"But she's right," said Harker. "You were watching her."

"Watching is not the same as checking someone out."

"I agree with Adrian," said Alison. "I watch my nephews and I'm definitely not checking them out." She grimaced. "They're eight and ten."

"But they aren't in a bar." Ellie was getting behind this logic. "If I see a guy staring, repeatedly"—she sent Adrian a look—"at an attractive woman in a bar, I'd say he was checking her out. He may be looking at her because she looks familiar or because he thinks she stole his dog, but no matter what he is watching her intently." She wanted to pat herself on the back. No one could argue with that logic.

"I wasn't watching her intently. I was keeping an eye on her to make sure she stayed out of trouble."

"Keeping an eye on her would constitute checking her out, even if it's in a non-sexual way, if you ask me," said Harker.

"I didn't," snapped Adrian.

"But I am," said Ellie. "I call for a vote."

"She wasn't wrong," said Harker.

"Two against one," she said.

All eyes fell on Alison.

"Alison come on. You don't check out your nephews. You're on my side, right?" Adrian smiled sweetly at her.

Alison frowned. "Sorry. She has a point with intently. I don't intently stare at my nephews."

"I wasn't..." He glanced around the table. "Damn it."

"Ha." She'd won and she was thrilled. She loved winning but more than that she loved irritating Adrian.

CHAPTER 7: ADRIAN

Adrian wasn't giving up. He'd spent the last week thinking about Ellie and all of tonight flirting with her. He needed her in his bed, naked and panting for him. His tequila-soaked brain stumbled over conversations, looking for a lie that he could prove.

"Poor baby is going to go home with nothing but his hand tonight." Ellie patted his cheek.

"That was rude." Alison handed her the bottle. "Drink."

Ellie wrinkled her face.

"Maybe she should switch to water," suggested Harker.

"No." Alison leaned across Adrian, hugging Ellie. "You're fine, right?"

"Yep." Ellie hugged her back, both of them resting on Adrian's chest. "You're the best friend ever. I love you."

"I love you too," said Alison. "Now, put on your big girl panties and take that drink."

"Right." Ellie leaned away slightly, tipping the bottle to her mouth.

"That's it." Adrian's synopses in his brain finally sputtered to life. "She said my sister was my girlfriend and she was definitely wrong about that." He'd won. She couldn't talk her way out of this one. His hand landed on her ass. It was his tonight, every lush inch. He grinned down at her, but his smile fled as tequila flew from Ellie's mouth straight at him.

CHAPTER 8: ELLIE

Ellie stared horrified at Adrian. His eyes were closed, and tequila dripped down his face. "I'm so sorry. I didn't mean—"

"Now, *that* was rude," said Harker. "Drink twice."

"No." Adrian opened his eyes and snatched the tequila bottle. "No more."

A snort of laughter slipped through Alison's hand which was firmly clamped over her mouth. Ellie bit her lip. Laughing at Adrian at this moment wouldn't be a good idea, but a giggle worked its way up her throat.

"Don't you dare laugh." Adrian gave her a stern look as he grabbed a napkin from under his drink and wiped his face, but his eyes sparkled. "This isn't funny."

"And that's a lie," said Harker, a half-smile on his handsome face.

"I'm allowed to lie." Adrian tossed the wet napkin onto the table. "She's not."

"I am too. I'm just not allowed to be wrong and I'm not."

"You're wrong. Unbelievably wrong. You said Paige

was my girlfriend and that is so not true."

"I don't recall saying that." She lied. The thought of him and that young woman had made her stomach twist, saying the words had been like expelling something bitter.

"You did," said the other three together.

"No. I don't think I did." Everyone was drunk. Maybe she could convince them that they're wrong.

"You"—Adrian grabbed Ellie's chin, moving slowly toward her until his lips almost touched hers. She couldn't stop her mouth from opening slightly. She wanted this kiss, needed it.—"are a poor loser."

"What?" She couldn't believe he'd said that. She shoved his hand away from her face.

"You heard me." He leaned back on his seat.

"I am not. I just don't remember using the term girlfriend."

"You did," said Harker.

She glanced at her friend and Alison nodded.

"Fine. I'm not a poor loser. If all of you think I said it then I guess I'll take your word."

"Good." Adrian stood. "Let's go."

"No. Not yet." She wasn't ready to be alone with him. She wanted him but she also wanted this night to continue. "It's not midnight. There's still plenty of time for you to do something so annoying and stupid that those two will agree."

"Okay Cinderella but as soon as the clock strikes midnight, we leave." Adrian waved over the waitress. "There's been a slight...accident." He frowned at Ellie.

32

"Can I get more napkins and a glass of water?"

"Sure." The waitress handed him some napkins from her tray, her fingers brushing over his. "I'll be right back with the water." Her hand rested on his shoulder, sliding down his arm as she walked away, her bottom swishing in her short shorts.

This was so typical. Women were drawn to alpha males like flies to shit and Ellie was done pretending she didn't notice the flirting. She refused to get involved with another cheater. Fortunately for her she had a lifetime of dealing with alpha a-holes. She knew exactly how to press their buttons and make them show their true jerkiness to everyone. She stood.

"Where are you going?" asked Adrian.

"To dance." She loved to dance. She hadn't gone out on the floor earlier because Alison hated dancing and then she'd been having fun with their game. Now, Alison had plenty of company and the quickest way to make a caveman act like a caveman was to make him jealous. Every guy she'd ever dated seemed to live by the belief that they could flirt and fuck other women, but their woman had better not even look at another guy. She was definitely going to do more than look.

"Sounds good." He stood.

"You're not invited."

"Ouch," said Harker. "And I thought Alison was mean."

CHAPTER 9: ADRIAN

A battle surged inside Adrian between desire, frustration and anger as he watched Ellie dance. She was sexy as fuck and every guy in here saw it. She'd started dancing in the crowd by herself but that'd lasted all of two seconds before the men had zeroed in on her like heat seeking missiles. She was the hottest thing at the club, her body swaying with the music, her chest heaving and her ass shaking in that short, tight, blue dress.

Three things kept him from barreling onto the dance floor, throwing her over his shoulder and leaving. First, he had too many sisters. He knew that'd do nothing but start a fight and probably not one that ended with him having sex. Second, she was only dancing and didn't seem interested in any of her partners. Third, even he knew Alison and Harker would consider it arrogant and stupid if he charged out there and he wasn't sure she'd go home with him if he lost this bet.

"You're either the most patient man I know or you're a ball-less coward," said Harker as soon as Alison excused herself to go to the restroom.

He barked a half-assed laugh. "I don't have much choice here."

"You have a ton of choices."

"Like what?" He glanced at the other man but only for a second because it was impossible for him to not watch Ellie.

"Personally, I'd drag her off the floor."

"If I do that, she'll insist on a vote. You're telling me that you'll side with me?" Perhaps he might be able to end this torture sooner than he'd thought. "That you'd say it wasn't stupid of me to do that?"

"Probably not, but sometimes stupid is necessary and it'd be worth it."

"Not to me." He wasn't risking tonight.

"At least she wouldn't be rubbing her ass all over some other guy's cock."

His teeth ground together. Ellie wasn't grinding…much, but it had happened, and he'd barely stayed sitting. "And if I did that, she wouldn't be rubbing anything of mine."

"You could join her." Alison sat back down at the table.

"I wasn't invited, remember?"

"Ellie doesn't own the dance floor," said Alison.

"True but I can't dance." His sisters had made fun of him for years about that. Making Ellie laugh at him was not going to get him laid.

"Then why were you going out there earlier?" asked Alison.

He shrugged. "The song was slow. I figured I could just hold her and sway, but I can't dance to this music." The song was fast and upbeat.

"Neither can they," said Harker. "They're not dancing; they're dry humping."

The guy had a point.

"That's not entirely true," said Alison. "The women dance. The men just stand there humping like the dogs they are."

"You're right." Harker laughed.

"Oh my god." Alison grabbed her phone and turned on the video, holding it toward her. "Today is December 31st and Gus—"

"Don't call me that," growled Harker.

"Gus," she said louder. "Admitted that I was right."

Adrian stood. He wasn't sitting here another minute listening to these two while Ellie rubbed some guy off with her ass.

"Going to dance?" asked Harker.

"Can't dance but I can dry hump with the best of them."

CHAPTER 10: ELLIE

Ellie couldn't take her eyes off Adrian as he walked toward her, maneuvering like a predator through the crowd of swaying people. His lips were tight with anger and his eyes were narrowed. It wouldn't take much to push him into asshole territory and free her from that stupid bet.

All she had to do was move closer to one of the three guys dancing with her and rub her ass against them. Adrian was already pissed. That'd be enough to make him cause a scene. She backed up a little, her gaze locking with Adrian's as he approached. His eyes were dark green and intense, heating her blood and making her insides throb. She quit inching toward the sweaty guy behind her and stayed where she was, swaying seductively as she waited for him.

He stopped in front of her, his breathing heavy and his body tense. She braced herself for his anger as he leaned down by her ear. "I can't dance."

He had to be kidding. Men like him were good at everything…everything but being faithful.

"Come back to the table with me." He took her hand.

"No." She pulled free and continued to dance, letting the music guide her body.

One of the other men, sensing the competition, danced closer, gyrating his hips next to hers. She watched Adrian over the other guy's shoulder, waiting for the explosion but although his jaw looked like it could crack a boulder, all he did was step up behind her and lean from side to side. His feet moved like he was stomping the earth to put out a fire.

He had to be joking. No one had that little rhythm. She spun around and the nervousness and uncertainty in his eyes told her he wasn't kidding. The man really could not dance.

She took his hands, placing them on her waist. "Follow my lead."

The relief on his handsome face made her heart melt but she couldn't have that, not with him. It'd be too dangerous. However, he was a friend of sorts and she wasn't a cruel person. The least she could do was to help him not embarrass himself.

She put her hands on his, keeping them in place as she turned, backing closer to him. He swayed with her, a bit clunkily but better than on his own.

He leaned down by her ear, his hands tightening on her waist. "Thank you."

His hot breath teased her neck and made her shiver. He must've noticed, or maybe he didn't. All she knew for sure was that he pulled her closer until her butt rubbed against him with each motion. She rotated her hips, teasing his rising cock. It felt big and hard and so good pressed against her ass. She raised her arms over her head, skimming her hands into his thick hair. She was drunk and horny, and she wanted this man.

His hands moved up from her waist, stopping right below her breasts as his lips tickled her neck, making her back arch and her ass grind against his cock. He pulled her closer and the ache between her legs became almost unbearable. She wanted to stroke herself or better yet, have him do it. She grabbed his hand sliding it down her chest and over her abdomen, stopping on her stomach.

"Should I touch you?'" His words were a harsh whisper in her ear. "Is that what you want? Here on the dance floor. My hand under your dress. My fingers slipping inside you." His hand moved to her hip, sliding downward along her thigh until his hot, rough fingers teased along the flesh where her dress stopped. "Answer me. Do you want me to touch you?" He nipped her ear and her hips arched backward, pressing her ass harder against his erection.

She turned her face until her lips were barely a breath away from his. "Yes."

His hand slid up her leg, moving inward, closer and closer to where she ached. She leaned against him, opening her legs a little as her hips rotated against his dick. His fingers skimmed across her pussy when someone slammed into them.

"Ellie, Ellie! It's almost midnight." Alison grabbed Ellie's arm, yanking her from Adrian's grasp. "We have champagne. Come on." Alison dragged her through the crowd. "Are you crazy?" she asked in a harsh whisper.

"What do you think you were doing? You can't let him feel you up on the dance floor. What's wrong with you?"

Her friend was right. She'd lost her mind or more accurately drowned it in a gallon of tequila. She stumbled after Alison, glancing back at Adrian through the crowd. He was not a happy man.

CHAPTER 11: ADRIAN

Adrian followed after Ellie, ready to throttle Alison. He stopped at the table where Harker stood filling champagne glasses.

"Here." Harker handed one to Ellie.

Alison grabbed one too, tossing it back before reaching for the bottle of champagne.

"You want more?" Harker yanked it away from her. "Ask nicely."

"You're an ass." Alison put her glass on the table and took Harker's full one.

Adrian stopped behind Ellie, pulling her back into his arms where she belonged.

"You still have a few minutes to find your partner for that midnight kiss," said the DJ over the music.

"I've got mine and I'm ready for a kiss and everything else." That last part was more than obvious with his erection pressing against that sexy ass of hers.

"Yeah. Uh." Ellie moved away from him.

"What's wrong now?" He'd about had it with her hot and cold routine.

"Nothing." She smiled at him, but it was forced. "I...I've had a little too much to drink."

"Me too. So what?"

She touched his arm with the tips of her fingers. "I...I think that I should go home."'

"Great. I'll go with you." He moved closer to her. She wasn't going to bail on him, not tonight, not after rubbing that lush ass against his cock for the last fifteen minutes.

"Alone. I'm drunk."

"Too drunk to keep your word?"

"What?"

"You agreed to go home with me." He wasn't a fan of blackmail but all's fair in sex and war.

"Ah...I know but..." She moved closer to him, her voice lowering, "What we almost did on the dance floor, that's not me."

"It sure felt like your ass rubbing against my dick." He almost groaned as the words left his lips. This wasn't the way to handle her but apparently, he didn't have any blood leftover for brain functions.

"You are such an ass." She stepped away from him.

"And you have a great one." He tried to back pedal, but she wasn't buying it.

"Go away."

"Ellie, don't do this." He caught her arm before she could walk away.

"Only a few seconds before the countdown starts. Grab your lover. Grab your friend. Just grab someone," shouted the DJ. "Because the New Year is almost here."

"Get away from me." She pulled free.

"Come on." He'd waited all night to be with her. He was at least getting this kiss. "You need me." He smiled his most charming smile and moved closer to her.

"I do not."

"Ten," shouted the DJ.

"You do."

"Nine." The crowd joined the DJ for the countdown.

"Who are you going to kiss?" he asked.

"Eight."

"It's too late to find someone else." He was her only option.

"Seven."

"It's not that late." Her eyes darted around the crowd.

"Six."

He grinned. Everyone had already paired off.

"Five."

"It looks like it's just me and you." He stepped closer to her.

"Four."

She frantically searched the crowd. He was starting to get insulted.

"Three."

"It's only a kiss." He turned her toward him. "One quick kiss."

"Two."

He lowered his head. He had every intention of making this one hot kiss that'd start here and end in his bedroom.

"One! Happy New Year!" shouted the crowd.

She was his. He reached for her, but she spun around, grabbing Alison and kissing her.

CHAPTER 12: ELLIE

When Ellie let go of Alison her friend's eyes were wide with shock. She wasn't sure which of them were more surprised by her impromptu kiss.

"I hadn't expected that," said Harker. "But I won't say I'm disappointed."

"I am," said Adrian. "If you're going to do something like that, do it right."

"What do you mean by that?" She turned toward him. His grin was sexy and devious and her body almost overheated because she knew she'd walked right into his trap.

"Let me show you." He pulled her into his arms and before she could protest, his mouth was on hers.

Suddenly, she had no idea why she'd been fighting this. It was perfect. It was meant to be. His arms tightened as she opened her lips and fell into his kiss. Her hands slid around his neck as she lifted onto her toes so she could fit her body more closely with his. She gasped softly against his mouth as his erection rubbed her mound. He cupped her ass, lifting her and pulling her closer as he groaned against her mouth. It was a rough sound of need that made wetness coat her panties

"Uhm." Alison tugged on Ellie's arm. "You're in the bar. In public."

Adrian inhaled deeply, causing his chest to rub against her breasts and sending tingles straight to the juncture between her legs. She clung to him even more. Right now, she didn't care where she was. All she wanted was to touch this man and have him touch her.

"Stop." Alison yanked on Ellie's arm. "This is almost as bad as the dance floor."

"She's right," Adrian said against her lips, putting her down on her feet and moving his hands to her waist. "Come home with me."

She was dizzy with passion and need but she took a deep breath. She shouldn't sleep with him again, but she wanted him way too much to deny herself now.

He cupped her face with both of his hands. "Please, come home with me. Not because of the bet but because you want to. Because you want me as much as I want you." His green eyes searched hers.

"So you're forfeiting the bet?" It didn't matter. She was going home with him, but she wanted to know if he'd actually give her the choice.

"Will you come home with me if I do?"

"Can't tell you that until you forfeit or force me." She shrugged. "Your choice."

"I'd never force you." His thumb caressed her lips. "The bet is off."

"Really?" She hadn't thought he'd do it. Alphas liked to win no matter what.

"Yes." His lips captured hers again, heating her blood to almost boiling before he let go and stepped away. "Your answer?"

She could barely think she was so hot for him. She had to clear her head to find some control. That was it. "On one condition."

"What?" Her eyes narrowed.

"I'm in charge. Completely. All night."

CHAPTER 13: ADRIAN

Adrian paid the Uber driver and almost dragged Ellie from the car. He was dying to touch more than her hand. If he'd driven to the bar, he probably would've fucked her in the parking lot.

"I mean it, Adrian." She followed behind him, almost running.

"Mean what?" He started up the stairs. Her legs were shorter than his and she was moving too slowly. They should've been in his apartment by now, naked or at least fucking. He tugged on her arm to hurry her along but she refused to move faster. It was probably her heels.

"I'm in charge."

"Sure. Whatever." He stopped, spinning around. He dropped her hand and bent, tossing her over his shoulder.

She squealed. "What are you doing?"

"Helping you." He secured her with his hand on her lush ass as he bounded up the stairs.

"I don't need help."

"Sure, you do." He pulled his keys from his pocket and unlocked his apartment.

"Put me down."

"Sure thing. You're the boss." He closed the door and let her slide down his body, keeping her pressed between him and the door. "Happy New Year, Ellie." He bent, his lips finding hers.

"Back up." She turned her head to the side, pushing on his chest but he didn't move.

"Why?" He kissed her cheek, his lips moving downward.

She moaned softly as he teased the sensitive skin where her shoulder met her neck. He pulled her closer, letting her feel how much he needed her. His hand found the hem of her dress, pushing it up and out of his way. Her skin was warm and soft as his fingers trailed between her legs to that softer place. That place that'd been made just for him.

"Stop." The word came out breathless, but her hand locked around his wrist.

"The worst word in the English language," he muttered as he used one hand to lean on the door, forcing his body away from hers. He left his other hand resting on her thigh. He couldn't deny himself that small touch. He'd been dreaming about this since Christmas.

"It isn't that bad." She laughed.

"Uh…Yeah, it is." He grabbed her hand and put it on his cock. "It's the worst thing you could say."

"Poor baby." She grasped him through his pants, squeezing.

He groaned, his cock growing. "Fuck, Ellie. That feels

so good."

"Does it?" She continued to stroke him.

"Yeah." His hand came off her thigh, moving to the button on his pants. These needed to go.

"Stop." She squeezed him, making him gasp.

"Why? I'm just trying to help you. These are definitely in the way." He needed her hot, little hand around his cock.

"I'm in charge." She stepped closer, stroking him. "Remember?"

"Yeah, right. Okay." Whatever she wanted to hear.

"Bedroom." She pushed him backward, hand still around his cock. "See, I don't need your tie."

"You've been leading me around by my dick since the first time I saw you smile," he said, earning another glorious squeeze.

As soon as they crossed the threshold to his room, she let him go and stepped to the side. Every instinct he had screamed for him to grab her, toss her on his bed and fuck her senseless but she wanted to be in charge and right now, he'd do whatever she wanted. So, he waited for her command.

She leaned against the wall, her eyes raking over him and making more blood rush to his dick. "Take off your shirt."

It was on the floor in less than a second.

Her gazed skimmed over his chest, stopping at his crotch. "Now, your pants."

He yanked off his shoes and socks.

"Slowly. I want you to tease me."

He was past teasing, but he took a deep breath and undid his belt and then the button. Her hot eyes stayed on his hands. He slowly lowered his zipper, sighing a bit at the release of pressure on his cock. He started to push his pants and underwear down.

"Leave the underwear."

"Wh…" He snapped his mouth shut and obeyed, arguing with her would slow this down. All he needed was for her to come close enough to touch and he'd take over this game.

Her eyes focused on his cock while his were on her face. Her cheeks were flushed with passion and her brown eyes were so dark they were almost black. Her mouth was slightly parted, and he groaned as her pink tongue darted out to wet her lower lip. He wanted that tongue on his cock and those lush, red lips wrapped around his dick. He stepped toward her.

"Stop." Her eyes lifted to his.

He hadn't meant to move but he wasn't stopping now. He took another step. "Ellie, I need you." And another. "Touch me, please."

CHAPTER 14: ELLIE

Ellie wanted nothing more than to do what Adrian asked. Her body needed to feel his against hers, inside hers.

"Please. I'm trying," he said as he continued walking toward her. "I'm asking nicely. I'm fucking begging you." He stopped so close to her that her breasts brushed against him with every breath.

She placed her hand on his chest, his heart racing under her fingertips. She ran it slowly downward, feeling the muscles twitch and tighten. Her eyes were locked with his, their lips almost touching. She skimmed her nail gently over his erection and he snapped. His mouth came down on hers, desperate and hungry. He pushed her against the wall as he shoved her dress up around her waist. She wrapped her legs around his hips, moaning against his mouth as his dick rubbed her pussy.

He unzipped her dress, pushing the top down and exposing her breasts. He growled as he moved her bra out of his way, his mouth devouring her flesh and sparking a fire that shot through her body. She rocked against him, her fingers sliding inside his underwear and wrapping her hand around his cock.

"Yes," he hissed against her skin before lifting his head and cupping her face. He held her still for his kiss, his tongue tangling with hers. His hands slid from her face down her body and between her legs, leaving a wake of fire wherever he touched. He shoved her underwear out of his way so his fingers could slide inside her. "I need you. Now."

"Condom." She nipped his lip. She was done waiting and teasing. She needed to fuck.

He stilled. "My wallet is in my pants. Shit." His hands slid under her ass. "Next time, I'm going to fuck you against the wall so hard we wake the neighbors." He turned and carried her to the bed and followed her down to the mattress. "Take off your underwear." He leaned over to the nightstand and grabbed a condom.

She didn't even think; she just obeyed, wiggling out of her dress and panties. He was back in a second, pushing his underwear down and kicking them aside as he tore open the wrapper with his teeth.

"Let me." She leaned up, reaching for his hand.

"Ellie, I can't."

"I'm in charge."

"Fine, but if I come in your hand, we'll both be fucking sorry."

"Then don't do it." She snatched the condom and grabbed his cock, her eyes darting to his at his sharp intake of breath. She rolled it slowly down his dick, loving the tension in his face. She was making this man, this alpha male, hard and desperate for her. She had him at her mercy, at least for the moment. She stopped at the base of his dick and squeezed.

"That's it." He shoved her hand away and spread her legs wide.

"Adrian, I'm in char…." The rest of the word turned into a moan as he slid inside her in one long, hard push. Her body tightened around him, welcoming him. This was what it'd wanted since she'd seen him walking toward her at the club.

He kissed her again as he began thrusting in a slow, steady rhythm that heated her blood. Her legs tangled with his and she wrapped her arms around his back, running her fingers down his spine all the way to his ass.

"Fuck," he groaned in her ear, his body moving faster. The soft brush of his chest hair on her nipples made them tighten and ache while his breath in her ear and his heart beating hard against her made her body tighten with need. She was getting close, so close. She closed her eyes, skimming her hands up and down his spine again but this time using her nails a little harder. It was like spurring a horse, because suddenly he grasped her hair, turning her face toward his as his hips rocked into her harder and faster. The sound of grunts, and flesh hitting flesh filled the air.

"Look at me." He bit her lower lip, pulling it into his mouth and sucking.

She gasped, opening her eyes. He was right there, his eyes so dark green they looked like the forest at midnight.

"You like this." He tightened his grip in her hair. "Admit it. No lies." His gaze bore into hers while his body commanded her and pushed her toward release. He let go of her hair and reached between her legs. "Truth. Ellie. The fucking truth."

"Adrian, please." She shifted, trying to get that finger on her clit but he danced around it.

"Admit it. Admit that this is better than fine. That this is fucking fantastic." His finger, slightly calloused, skimmed over her clit in a feather-light touch.

If he wasn't going to do this, she would. She reached between her legs, but he captured her hand.

"Oh, no you don't. This pussy is mine tonight." He kissed her again but there was no softness only dominance. "Mine. Say it."

"Yes. Please, Adrian." She'd say anything he wanted as long as he touched her.

"Yes, what?"

"Touch me." She'd hate herself for begging later, but right now it didn't matter.

"Say it." He teased her clit with his thumb, his cock sliding into her over and over.

"Yes. Please. It's great." Once the first words slipped out, she couldn't stop. The truth flowed from her. "God, you make me scream. No one has ever made me scream. This is the best sex I've ever had." She grabbed his hair, yanking on it. "Happy now?"

"Yeah." He couldn't look more smug if he tried.

"Then touch me. Please. Fucking touch me."

He did. His thumb pressed down on her clit as his mouth landed on hers and his body picked up its pace again, fucking her hard and fast and pushing her up that mountain. She clung to him, holding on for the ride because she had no other choice. Everything pulsed and tingled and tightened. His body plunged into hers over and over as his thumb rubbed her fast and hard. She tightened, clinging to him, her hips arching into his hand as she shattered, screaming as she came. He pumped into her again and again and then grunted and stilled as he came. His large body dropped on top of hers, his breath hot and heavy in her ear.

She ran her hand up and down his spine but not to entice, just to keep touching him. He was so warm and strong, but his skin was so soft.

"Keep doing that, and I'll be fucking you again in a minute," he grumbled into her ear.

"That'd be okay with me." She kissed the side of his head. She was tired of fighting with him, tired of denying that she wanted this man. Tonight, her pussy may belong to him but that meant his dick was hers—actually, his entire body was hers to command.

"I've changed my mind. It's not fine if we fuck again."

"Don't," he said as he pulled out of her, rolling to his back and depositing the condom in a wastebasket next to the bed.

"Don't what?

"Don't deny how good this was." His gaze captured hers. "Please. Not yet. Let's just enjoy this."

"I wasn't going to." She smiled softly at him. He looked so darn cute—annoyed and a little uncertain. "I'm sorry about saying that before."

"Why did you?"

"Because you were so cocky."

"You like that about me." His eyes dipped to his dick and his lips curled into a smile.

"That's not what I meant." She snuggled against his side. "What I was going to say was that once again you didn't let me be in charge."

"Sure, I did."

"You did not."

"Trust me." He kissed her. "I did the best I could. You'll have to accept that."

"Accept that?" Oh, she was so not going to accept that.

"I'll let you be in charge whenever you want for as long as I can take it. So next time, don't tease me all night and I'll probably be able to last longer before I'm done with the games." He kissed her again. "Now, I need some sleep." He rolled over.

"I mean it, Adrian. Next time, I'm in charge." She flopped down on her back.

"Sure, babe. Whatever you want."

"Do not call me that." She elbowed his side when he chuckled.

CHAPTER 15: ELLIE

Ellie woke and she had to pee. Bad. She shoved the covers down and got out of bed, stumbling through the dark bedroom.

"Ouch." She grabbed her foot, hopping in place. She'd stepped on Adrian's belt buckle. The curtains were closed in the bedroom, but faint moonlight filtered in from the large window in the living room. She kicked the pants aside and made her way out of the room. Last time, she'd been here she'd used the bathroom in his bedroom but there had to be another one. She wasn't risking her toes any more than she had to. She stopped in the living room, looking around. She hadn't paid too much attention to the place on Christmas.

It was a typical apartment. Kitchen. Living room. Balcony and two closed doors. One of them had to be a bathroom. She took a step and hesitated. She was pretty sure he lived alone but not sure enough to run around naked. She peered into the bedroom, trying to see anything in the darkness. Her dress was dark blue, and Adrian had worn black pants and a gray shirt that'd brought out the green of his eyes. She couldn't see anything but a laundry basket on the floor by the door with a glaringly white shirt in it. It was rumpled but it couldn't be that dirty. She grabbed the shirt and pulled it on, hurrying across the house before she peed on the floor. She carefully opened the first door.

"Thank you. Thank you." She hurried inside the bathroom.

When she was done, she made her way back to the bedroom. She stopped at the door. It was so dang dark all she could make out was a large form on the bed. She moved carefully across the room, bumping into a shoe and almost falling. That was it. She needed a light of some sort. She did her best to stay by the wall as she made her way to the window. She tugged open the drapes just enough to let in some light.

She turned, her breath catching in her throat. Adrian was on his back his arms tossed above his head, covers piled haphazardly over his hips. The moon highlighted him like a god to be worshiped. His body was perfection, muscular but lean and his face was even more handsome in sleep—his jaw defined and cheekbones high. His lashes were long and dark, covering eyes she knew were the tempting color of emeralds. His lips were opened slightly and all she wanted to do was crawl up that body, rubbing against him like a cat.

She moved closer. Why shouldn't she? He'd woken her with sex. Even if he hadn't, she'd never met a man who minded a wake-up fuck. She moved closer. Right now, she could be in complete charge but only until he woke, unless…His arms were already over his head. Too bad he didn't have bed posts, but she could make it work. All she needed was something to tie his hands.

She snatched his pants from the floor and pulled out his belt. This would do.

CHAPTER 16: ADRIAN

Adrian woke with a start. Someone held his hands and was trying to tie them. His instincts and training kicked in before he had a chance to think. He grabbed his assailant by the hands and rolled.

Ellie's squeak made him pause. He stared down at her. Moonlight splashed across her face. She was gorgeous with her honey-brown hair mussed and her lips parted in surprise.

"Sorry. I thought I was being attacked." He settled his body more firmly against hers. "Maybe I was." He tugged on the belt that was still in her hands. "Were you going to tie me up?" His cock, which had been waking slowly from her softness beneath him, rose like a catapult.

"Yes." She smiled sheepishly at him. "I figured it was the only way I could really be in charge."

"Hmm." He shifted, rubbing his dick against her softness. "You sure you want to do that? You admitted that it's pretty damn good the way we've been doing it. The best you've ever had." He raised a brow at her. "And don't deny it."

"I can claim duress."

"Duress?" He laughed. "I don't think wanting to come qualifies as duress."

"It should. Now, get off me." She shoved at his chest.

"Why would I do that? I'm quite happy where I am." He rocked his hips and her eyes drifted half-closed. "And so are you." He needed to be inside her. He wanted to fuck her slowly this time, make her moan and sigh over and over. Make her say his name when he took her to the edge.

"No. Stop." She shoved on his chest again. "I mean it."

"No, you don't but I'll play." He rolled off her. "If you want to pretend to be in charge, that's fine."

"I'm not pretending." She sat up, holding the belt.

"The shirt looks good on you." His fingers trailed along where the material rested on her upper thigh.

"Thanks, now give me your hands."

"You're going to tie me up with the belt?" He shook his head. "Not a task for a novice."

"What do you suggest?" She hadn't been too sure how she was going to make it stay tight enough around his wrists.

"You're in charge. I don't want to overstep."

"I'm ordering you to tell me."

"Well, if I were going to tie you up"—his eyes skimmed over her body before he started unbuttoning her shirt—"first, I'd make sure you were naked."

"Stop that." She slapped his hand away. "You are naked. So, tell me what I should do."

"Unbutton the shirt or I won't talk."

"I'm in charge. You agreed."

"Consider it a negotiation." His fingers caressed her thigh. She was soft and warm. Her body wanted to follow his lead, but her mind fought him for every inch. It was fun and frustrating and so fucking hot when she finally surrendered.

"Fine. One button." She unhooked one button, causing the shirt to gape and exposing most of her luscious breasts. "What would you use to tie me up?"

"Let me show you." His finger grazed across the skin right above her nipple.

"No. I'm tying you up." Her voice was a little breathless.

"You sure? Have you ever done that?"

"No, but so what?"

"I can teach you and then, next time you can tie me up." He got out of the bed, flipped on a light and walked to his closet.

"How many women have you tied up?"

"Here?" He grinned at her over his shoulder. "None. At the Club? A few."

"Do you have the same equipment here?" She tried to see what he was getting from the closet.

"Nope but I know how to improvise." He pulled out a clean sheet and two neckties.

"That's a lot of…material."

"The sheet goes under the mattress. We can then attach the ties around your wrists and to the sheet."

"Your wrists. Not mine."

"You're going to insist on this aren't you?" He knew that stubborn tilt to the chin. It was universal to woman and it meant they weren't going be swayed by logic.

"Yes and leave the light on. I want to see you when I suck you dick."

Now, that he could get behind one hundred percent.

CHAPTER 17: ELLIE

"Are you sure about this?" Adrian sat on the bed his back against the headboard.

They'd slid the rolled-up sheet under the top part of the mattress before attaching one tie to each end. As soon as Ellie got his hands secured, he'd be at her mercy. Every inch of that six-foot, muscular body would be hers to tease, taunt and taste.

"Absolutely. I've never been more sure of anything." She got onto the bed and straddled him, his dick pressing against her leg. "Give me your hand."

"Promise not to leave me tied up." He held out his arm and she wrapped one of the ties around his wrist.

"I wouldn't do that." She tightened the knot and grabbed his other hand.

"I don't know. You're kind of mean." He kept his arm by his side.

"I'm not mean." She tugged on his hand, but she couldn't make him move.

"You lied and said sex with me was *fine*." He said it like it was vile.

"That was for your own good." She tugged on his arm again. "Come on. You agreed."

"Promise you'll be nice to me."

"I'll be very, very nice to you." She'd never be able to force his arm to the restraint, so that left persuasion. She sat back, rotating her hips and rubbing against his cock. "Please, Adrian."

"Men are fucking idiots." He stretched out his arm.

"You can be sometimes, but you do get a reward for obeying." She unbuttoned another button on her shirt. It was already big and with the other buttons already unfastened this one made it indecent and perfect for what they were getting ready to do.

"I may regret letting you tie me up later but right now, I can't imagine being anything but happy." His gaze was on her breasts as she leaned forward grabbing his wrist.

As soon as she had him tied up nice and tight, she got off him.

"Where are you going?"

"Worried?" She liked making him sweat a bit. It was good for him.

"A little but more horny."

"I see that." She stared at his erection, letting her tongue dart out to wet her lips. "What should I do about that?"

"I have a few suggestions but one's at the top of my list."

"You're lucky because I think it's at the top of my list too." She pulled up her hair, tying it in a makeshift bun.

"Fuck, yeah." He muttered, his dick growing before her eyes.

"I think it's time for a shower."

"Don't play with me, Ellie."

"Oh, Adrian. That's exactly what I'm going to do." She crawled back onto the bed, blowing softly over his hard cock.

CHAPTER 18: ADRIAN

Adrian's blood thudded in his ears as Ellie's warm breath teased the sensitive tip of his dick.

"What should I do first?" She stared up at him, her lips only centimeters away from the tip of his cock.

He ground his teeth together. He was pretty sure telling her to suck him would get him the exact opposite. His chest heaved as he forced himself to say, "Whatever you want. You're in charge." He almost choked on the words.

"You're learning." She smiled at him and his heart lurched.

This was the woman he wanted. The one he'd seen at the bar for that quick second or so when she was on the phone—her eyes alight with amusement and her smile wide and true.

"I think I should reward you for that." Her hand wrapped around his shaft. "What do you think?"

"Yes," he hissed as she squeezed.

"You are so agreeable." She blew on his dick, her eyes never leaving his as she slowly licked the tip of his cock.

His eyes drifted half-closed at the pleasure as she ran

her tongue up and down his length. "Fuck. Yes." He reached for her head, but his hands were tied. He slid down the headboard a bit, his hips lifting toward her mouth, begging her without words to take him inside.

She lowered her lips around his tip, pulling him into her wet heat and sucking. Her hands worked his shaft as her head bobbed.

"Fuck," he groaned as she took him deep, half-swallowing his cock. His hips thrust into her mouth, pushing his dick even deeper.

She pulled off him and he moaned, wanting more of that pleasure. He jerked on his restraints, trying to touch her head to keep her mouth on his cock but he couldn't fucking move.

She straddled his legs, bending down and capturing his lips. He leaned forward, spilling all his desperation into the kiss and she melted against him.

He needed to touch her, to hold her, to be in control. "Untie me." He said against her lips.

"No." She kissed along his cheek, moving downward.

"Come on. Please." He was done following. He was ready to lead.

"Nope," she whispered in his ear before nibbling on his neck.

He stared at her breasts as they swayed gently with her movements. "Take off your shirt." He needed to see those tits, touch them, taste them.

"No." She lowered her pussy to his cock, rubbing along his length.

"Fuck. That feels good." It did and it didn't. It was great but not enough.

"It does." She kissed him again, rocking against him and making his dick slick with her desire.

"Untie me. I can help." He kissed her ear. "I can touch your clit. Make you scream."

"No." She braced her hands on the headboard as her hips moved faster along his cock, teasing his tip with her heat and wetness.

He needed to be inside her while she rode him. He had to feel those hips rock as her pussy clung to him. He yanked again on his restraints, shaking the bed. He should've never agreed to this. "Damn it. Fuck."

She undid the buttons on her shirt, His temper eased as his gaze followed her fingers, waiting for those luscious breasts to be free. She shrugged off his shirt and leaned toward him, offering him her breast.

He clasped onto her nipple, sucking hard. Her hands tangled in his hair, holding him close as her pussy, hot and wet, rubbed against him. He bit down gently, and she moaned, arching her back, her hips moving faster. Her face was flushed and her eyes were closed. She was almost there. He rolled his hips thrusting hard against her. He wanted to see her come. See her break apart on top of him as she found her pleasure, but she stopped, lifting away.

"Babe, wait. What's wrong? Why'd you stop?"

"Don't call me that." She kissed her way down his chest, licking along his abdomen. He tensed, watching that honey-brown head move between his legs and waiting for her mouth.

"Yeah, that's it," he said as she kissed the tip of his dick before sliding him between her lips. His hips thrust at the feel of all that wet heat surrounding his cock. "Fuck."

Her head bobbed as she sucked him, each time going deeper. He groaned as his dick pressed against her throat. She gagged a bit, pulling off and then was right back swallowing him as her hand worked his staff, squeezing and pulling.

"Stop." His balls tightened and his legs shook. "I'm gonna come. Stop."

She lifted off him, her eyes watery. "Condom."

CHAPTER 19: ELLIE

"Nightstand." Adrian's voice was gravely with need.

Ellie leaned forward, pressing her hip against his erection as she opened the top drawer. She grabbed a condom and then straddled him again. She tore open the package and began to slowly roll it down his cock, loving how he trembled at her touch.

"Babe hurry up. Please."

"I told you not to call me that. Now, I'm taking my time." She hated being called babe. Men used terms of endearment to disguise the fact that they fucked so many different women, they couldn't remember their names. He may be funny and charming but deep down he was the same type of man as Marc. The only difference was that this time she was in charge. She pulled the condom off him.

"What are you doing?" He almost growled.

"Giving you exactly what guys like you want." She paused. "Actually, all guys but especially men like you." She lowered her mouth to his cock, taking him deep inside as her fingers gently squeezed his balls.

"Fuck. Don't. Fu...ck." The words were interrupted by

pants as his hips thrust into her mouth. "I…can't…"

She sucked harder and he moaned, his cum spilling into her mouth in hot spurts.

CHAPTER 20: ADRIAN

Adrian had never been more confused. He was both satiated and furious. Ellie leaned over him, her soft breasts resting against his chest as she lowered her head to kiss him.

"Untie me."

"What's wrong?" She stilled, obviously sensing his mood from his tone.

"Untie me. Now."

"Okay." She moved off him, her fingers grappling with the knot. "What's the matter?" She gave him a smug look. "I know you liked it."

Liked it? Hell, he'd fucking loved it and yet, he was pissed. He hadn't wanted to come like that, not this time. The restraint loosened around his wrist and he slipped his hand free. She moved to the other side of the bed, her warm body pressing against his.

"I got it." He shifted, blocking her with his back as he untied his other hand.

"Adrian, what's wrong?"

He had no idea so he didn't say anything. His emotions

were as tight and tangled as the knot around his wrist. The bed shifted slightly, and he glanced over his shoulder. Ellie stood, gathering her clothes.

"What the fuck are you doing?"

"Leaving."

"Don't." His fingers worked faster at the knot.

She pulled on her panties and bra.

"Ellie, get back in bed." He was pissed but he didn't want her to go.

"Why? So, you can snap at me or ignore me? No thanks. I get plenty of that at home."

"What the hell does that mean?"

"It doesn't matter." She stepped into her dress, pulling it up over her lush body before heading for the door.

"Wait. Please." He tugged at the knot with his teeth. "I can't get this untied." He wasn't lying. The damn thing was stuck.

She stopped in the doorway, looking back at him.

"Don't leave me like this." He meant more than being restrained.

She frowned but walked back to the bed, her small fingers pushing his out of the way as she fiddled with the knot.

He should say something, but he was still too angry with her. *Guys like him.* She barely knew him. He barely knew her, but he'd treated her with nothing but respect. Hell, he'd even let her tie him up and she still gave him this shit.

The knot loosened.

"There. You should be able to get it now." She strode toward the door.

"Wait." His fingers unraveled the cloth.

She ignored him.

He loosened the tie and pulled his hand free. He hopped out of bed, hurrying across the room and catching her in the living room. "Don't go."

She stopped but wouldn't meet his eyes. "Look it was fun."

"Don't say that." He moved closer. This was more than fun. She had to feel it too.

"It wasn't fun? Is that what you'd rather hear?" This time she met his gaze, but her eyes were hard, and he was pretty sure she was close to crying.

"Please don't go." He took her hand. "I can't...I don't know how to...I'm sorry." That was the simplest explanation.

"For what? For not liking the blow job?" She shook her head, a look of confusion on her face. "Although, you did seem to like it enough to finish."

"That wasn't it." He pulled her to the couch and sat. "I loved that. You know I did."

"Then why are you being such a dick."

"I don't know." He leaned back, dropping his head against the top of the couch. "I'm used to being in control. I wanted to be inside you. I wanted you to come too."

"You were inside me."

He glanced at her, grinning slightly. "True, but you know what I mean."

76

"It was my decision. My choice."

"But you didn't come."

"My choice." She shrugged.

"Stay. I can fix that for you."

She studied him a long time and then shook her head, pulling her hand from his. "I should go. I have a ton of things to do."

"Like what." He stood too. "I'll help. I don't have to work today."

"I don't think that'd be a good idea."

"It'd be a great idea." He moved closer, pulling her into his arms. "We could work and play." He wanted to spend the day with her, a lot of days and nights.

"Marc would love that."

"Marc?" He stiffened.

"Yeah. I'm packing his things."

"You're still with him?" This was unbelievable.

"No." She pulled away from him. "I'm not *with* him."

"Why are you helping him pack?" He told himself to remain calm, to keep his cool but it was a waste of time.

"Because I want him out of my apartment."

"So, you are still with him."

"No. I'm not. We're not a couple. We're not sleeping together."

"But you're still living together."

"It's only been a week since we broke up. He hasn't found a place yet."

"Has he tried?" The only reason that guy hadn't left was because he believed they'd get back together.

"Yes." Her chin tipped up in defiance—almost in challenge.

"Liar." He wanted to shake some sense into her.

"How am I supposed to know what he does or doesn't do? He says he's looking."

He didn't want to ask. He didn't want to know but he had to. "Are you still sleeping in the same bed." This would either set him off or calm him down a degree or two.

"No. I'm sleeping on the couch."

"*You're* on the couch?" That guy was the biggest ass he'd ever met, and he'd met some real jerks in the service.

"He refused to move out of the bed."

"Why the fuck are you putting up with this?" He didn't even give her a chance to answer. "You know what? You're not. I'm going over there and tossing his ass out."

"No, you're not. I'll handle this."

She was fuming, and he should've known to stop, to let this go—for now—but his temper was hot and that set off his mouth.

"Like you've handled it so far?"

"It's only been a week," she repeated.

"You want to get back together with him." It all made sense now. That was why she didn't want to see him, except when they fucked. She was still hung up on her ex.

"Marc and I are over. He cheated on me. I'll never get back together with him." Her face scrunched up. "You really think I'd do"—she waved her hand between them—"what we've done if I wanted to get back with Marc?"

"Yeah, women like you do it all the time." He'd see

how she liked being classified with all other sucky-women.

"Women like me?" Apparently, she liked it about as much as he did because her eyes widened in surprise, like she was astonished he'd dare to say that.

"Yeah. Women who date or fuck guys like me."

"You know what? You're right." She grabbed her purse. "I'm done. With you. Marc. And all alpha a-holes. I'm done with every last one of you."

"Except your live-in boyfriend." He followed her to the door and stopped. "Give me a second to grab my pants."

"Why?"

"To take you home. You don't have a car."

"I'll call an Uber." She pulled her phone out of her purse.

"I'll drive you."

"No."

He snatched her phone from her hands. "Yes. It's the least I can do for nutting in your mouth."

CHAPTER 21: ELLIE

Ellie grabbed her phone and left, slamming the door behind her but even that didn't block Adrian's shout. She didn't care. She was so freaking done with guys like him. She swallowed a lump in her throat. She'd known better, but she'd still gone home with him. She opened the Uber app.

"Ellie, wait. Fucking stop." Adrian caught up with her at the end of the hallway.

She ignored him, continuing down the stairs into the parking lot. She tapped the app again. "Damn it. Don't do this to me." She just couldn't win today. She held up the phone, searching for a better signal, one the app could use to find her location.

"You're not taking an Uber." Adrian followed behind her.

She glanced around. She had no idea of the address or even the name of the apartment complex.

"Get in." Adrian opened his car door. "We don't have to talk. Just get in the fucking car."

There wasn't a street sign anywhere. She was so angry

she almost broke her finger, closing the app. She walked over to his car. "Don't speak to me. Ever."

"That works for me."

"You spoke." She got into the car, yanking the door from his grasp.

He got into the driver's side, slamming his door. He didn't even look at her as he started the car and pulled out of the parking lot, heading toward her apartment.

Good. He remembered where she lived so there was no reason to speak. She stared out the window. This wasn't how she'd wanted tonight to end.

She'd planned on a fun night with Alison and then back to the apartment to pack up Marc's stuff before he came home. Those plans had changed as soon as Adrian had sauntered over to their table. Nothing had mattered except being with him. She was so stupid.

From today forward she was one hundred percent done with men like him. She'd already started a small flirtation with a guy from the human resource firm in the office building where she worked. He was nice and kind of cute. Unfortunately, she felt nothing for him but fondness.

She glanced at Adrian. He had dressed in a worn pair of jeans and a black T-shirt. There was something seriously wrong with her because even though he was being an ass she still wanted to tear off those clothes and cover his body with kisses.

He pulled his Mustang into her apartment complex and parked, opening the door to get out.

"I'm fine. Thanks for the....thanks." She got out of the

car.

He followed her toward the building.

She stopped. "Go home."

"I guess you don't learn."

"You're talking to me."

"The ride is over," he said.

"It most certainly is." She continued toward her building and he followed. As soon as she stepped inside the foyer, she turned, blocking the door. "Good night."

"I'll walk you to your door."

"I'm fine in here."

"You don't know that."

"I've lived here for years."

"I don't care." His jaw was tight, and his mouth drawn in a thin line. "I'm making sure you get to your apartment safe and sound."

She shook her head. Arguing with men like him was pointless. She walked through the entranceway and pressed the button on the elevator. They both stepped inside and rode to her floor in silence. She didn't even bother telling him to stay in the elevator. There was no reason to waste her breath. She stopped at her door, Adrian right behind her. She was glad he wasn't trying to talk to her, but she didn't like a huge, moody gorilla-man nipping at her heels.

She pulled her key out of her purse and opened the door. "Goodbye, Adrian."

He turned and strode back to the elevator. She closed the door behind her, bracing herself to deal with Marc but the house was quiet. She leaned against the door, fighting back tears. Why did she always fall for assholes? Not that she'd fallen for Adrian, but she'd been heading in that direction and she still had no idea why he'd gotten so upset. There was no way he didn't like the blow job. She was good at those.

It didn't matter. Today was a new year and a new beginning for her. She was going to find a nice man who wasn't all about working out and chest pounding his physical superiority over everyone else. She was done with man-brutes, especially Adrian.

CHAPTER 22: ADRIAN

It was after one in the afternoon when Adrian woke, still in a foul mood. He showered, grabbed something to eat and flopped down on the couch to watch TV. He flipped through the stations, too restless and pissed to watch anything. He'd let her tie him up, but he was still a *guy like that*. She barely knew him, but she'd already labeled him and stuffed him neatly in a box. Fuck her. He'd never been one of those guys like her ex. He'd never treated a woman like crap for any reason. *Until last night.*

He dropped his head back against the couch. She'd sucked him off and he'd been an ass. Just the memory of that blow job had his cock stiffening—her kneeling between his legs, her lips wrapped around his dick as her eyes stared into his. Fuck. He had to stop thinking of her or he'd have to masturbate. The problem was he didn't want to stop thinking of her and he definitely didn't want to jerk-off, not when he knew a gorgeous, sexy as sin woman who wanted him too. He grabbed his jacket and keys and headed to his car.

Adrian knocked on Ellie's door, half-hoping Marc was there. He'd love to kick the guy's ass. Of course, that'd only confirm Ellie's perception of him.

Ellie opened the door, her hair pulled back in a messy ponytail that made him want to wrap it around his hand as he fucked her from behind. They could do it right here in the doorway. No one was around. The hallway was empty.

"What are you doing here?" She held money in her hands and the look on her face wasn't surprised glad-to-see him. It was more surprised and annoyed.

He probably deserved that look but he could change that. "Ah…I thought we could go grab something to eat and talk."

"I've got pizza coming."

"Great. I love pizza." He grinned, trying his best to charm her.

"Adrian, I don't think this is a good idea."

"Why?"

"It isn't going to work."

That wasn't what he wanted to hear. "Come on. Give me another chance. I'm sorry about last night."

"This isn't about last night, although I have no idea what made you so mad."

"Let me in so we can talk. Just talk. I promise." He meant it, kind of. He wouldn't argue if the conversation led to something else.

"No. Marc might come home anytime."

"Home?" He held up his hand. "Sorry. Forget I said that." He was going to have a hard time forgetting that she still referred to this as Marc's home, but he'd fight that fight later. The mission right now was getting her to talk to him. Be with him. "Let's go somewhere. There's a new coffee shop around the corner. We could both make everyone nervous when we ordered tea instead of coffee." Another smile but it was like trying to charm a statue.

"I have a lot to do—"

"I'll help. My day is free." He stepped a bit closer, hoping she'd back up and give him nonverbal permission to enter her apartment.

"Sorry. It wouldn't be good for you to be here when Marc comes back. He'll be hung over and bitchy. Having you here won't help."

"I can handle it." His fingers tightened into a fist. "And I won't start anything." He'd finish it though if the other guy was a jerk to her.

"But he will and he's an MMA instructor."

It was like she'd slapped him. All this time he'd assumed she was worried about Marc or a fight in her house, but she was worried about him. Him. "I can handle myself."

"Oh." She almost touched his arm but dropped her hand. "I'm sure you can but he's a professional and—"

"I can handle myself," he repeated. He had extensive hand-to-hand combat training. He wasn't some punk off the streets. "I was in the Marines for ten years."

"I'm not saying…Look, none of that matters."

"It does to me."

"This"—she waved her hand between them—"isn't going to work."

"Why? Because you don't think I can handle myself in a fight?"

"No." She gave him a disgusted look. "I've been with Marc for almost three years. I thought we were going to get married and have kids. The whole deal. I'm not ready to jump into a relationship or to start dating right now." This time she did touch his arm. "Thank you for everything but please, I need time to get things sorted out."

Time. He didn't like it, but he'd wait. "Okay." He leaned down and kissed her on the forehead. "I can give you time." He forced himself to take a step back. "If you need anything, give me a call." If she didn't call him in a few weeks, he'd call her because this wasn't over.

CHAPTER 23: ADRIAN

Adrian's phone rang as he grabbed a tube of toothpaste from the store shelf. It was Mitch. "Hey, what's up."

"Are you going to the gym today?"

"Already been there." He was a morning person. He liked to get his workouts done early.

"You disgust me. How in the hell do you get up so early on a Saturday? No, not how…Why? We were out late last night."

"Because I'm not a lazy ass like you." He pushed his cart out of the aisle. "Plus, I don't drink as much as you do. It's easier to wake up without a hangover that way. You should try it."

"One day when I'm old like you."

He laughed, slowing down as he passed the stationary aisle.

"What are you doing later? I'm going to the gym but do you wanna meet for lunch and a game of pool at Murphy's?"

"Sure. I have to stop at the coffee shop first." He pushed his cart down the aisle filled with party supplies, stopping in front of the wrapping paper section.

"Coffee shop? You don't drink coffee."

"It's Paige's first day on the job. I thought I'd go in and see how she's doing."

"Harass her more like it."

"Of course." He chuckled. He had no idea what kind of wrapping paper Ellie would like. It was mid-January, so the Christmas stuff was gone but he liked this blue one. It had little green flowers on it.

"What are you doing now?"

"Picking up groceries." He glanced around. It wouldn't surprise him to find out that Mitch was watching him. Unlike a normal person, if Mitch saw someone he knew in a store, he'd call and follow them around. The guy couldn't help hunting someone or something whenever he got the chance.

"Groceries?" Mitch didn't believe him.

"Where are you?" He scanned the area but couldn't find his friend.

"Jesus. You're looking at wrapping paper again, aren't you?"

"Get your ass out here and show yourself."

"I'm in my car." He must've opened the door or something because a beep sounded repeatedly followed by the slam of a car door. "I'm not following you, but I know you."

"Not well enough because I'm not looking at wrapping paper." He dropped the blue one with flowers and a pink one with glitter into his cart.

"Bullshit. Fucking call the woman before your balls fall off and your dick turns into a pussy."

"You don't think it's too soon?" He'd been wanting to call Ellie since the day she told him she needed time, but he had to do this right. Too soon and he'd be annoying. Too late and she could be seeing someone else.

"I think it's already too late."

"Really? Wait a minute. How would you know? You don't even know what she looks—"

"Too late for you, dumbass. You're whipped."

"I am not." He just missed her. It was funny because he barely knew her, but he wanted to know her better.

"Call her and ask her out but don't tell her you've been picking out wrapping paper for her or you'll scare the poor woman away."

"I should've lied to you."

"You should've never bought it. You're turning into some besotted teenage girl."

His biggest regret in life was not hiding that paper when Mitch had come over. Over the last few weeks, he'd been grabbing a package or two when he went to the store. He planned on giving it to her at some point after they started dating.

"Call her or give me her number and I'll call her. I'll tell her to give it up at least one more time so my friend can grow his balls back."

"You're not calling her." He passed an aisle where a woman was setting up a display of heart-shaped boxes. That was it. "And neither am I, until Valentine's Day."

CHAPTER 24: ELLIE

Ellie took a sip of her tea, making a face. It was cold and slightly bitter. She should order another one or maybe even something to eat. She'd been hiding at the coffee shop for over three hours. Today, Marc would discover that she hadn't paid his share of the rent for the health club where he was co-owner.

She'd told him right after they'd broken up that she was done paying his bills, but the man didn't seem to believe her. She couldn't blame him because she continued to pay the utilities and the Internet bill but she needed those things. She'd thought when she'd removed herself from their joint account, he'd get the hint, but he hadn't. Probably because the bank account wasn't empty yet.

Today, the truth of his situation would come crashing down on him. She'd paid all the bills since they'd moved in together. His check had been deposited into the joint account, but it was less than twenty-five percent of her paycheck. He'd grown accustomed to spending her money.

She wasn't looking forward to the coming confrontation, hence why she was hiding in the coffee shop until he cooled down. Maybe, just maybe this would be the catalyst he needed to actually move out. Even if it didn't, he'd have to leave soon. They'd signed a month-to-month lease in December and it was up on Monday. She'd sign the new lease and Marc would have to go.

She picked up her cup and put it down. She wasn't drinking any more of this. It was time for a Coke. She closed her laptop and started to stand, freezing half-off her seat as Adrian walked into the shop.

CHAPTER 25: ADRIAN

Adrian walked into the coffee shop. He'd grab a drink, say hi to his sister and leave. It'd been nice outside when he gotten home from the store, so he'd decided to walk but now the storm clouds gathered overhead. He had no desire to be stuck at the coffee shop or caught in the downpour.

He got in line. This place was busy, but the line was moving fast. Paige was doing a good job. Not that he'd expected anything else. They'd all been raised to work hard. The guy in front of him stepped aside, coffee in hand and Adrian walked up to the register. She looked so cute behind the counter in her green and brown uniform.

"Hi, may I…What are you doing here?" Paige's smile turned into a frown.

"I'm thirsty." He hadn't thought she'd hug him, but he hadn't quite expected her to be this irritated by his presence. Days when he could innocently annoy his sisters were good days.

"You don't drink coffee."

"You sell other things."

She rolled her eyes. "What do you want?"

"Is this how you treat all your customers?"

"Only the annoying ones."

He laughed. "I'll take an iced tea. No sugar. Add lemon."

"We have an orange tea that's terrific."

"Okay. I'll try that." He handed her the money. "How's it going?"

"Great. I love it here."

Now, he wanted to roll his eyes. Everyone said that the first day on the job. "Good but when you don't love it stick with it." Paige was a bit flightier than the rest of them. Spoiled was the word his other sisters would use.

"I don't need a lecture." She began preparing his drink.

"I think you do."

"Your friend is here."

"See. This is what I'm talking about. You don't give it your all. I know you can do better than that to avoid the sage advice from your favorite brother."

"I'm not trying to avoid your stupid advice." She made a face at him. "I'm trying to be a good sister." Her saccharin tone could put him into a sugar coma.

"Right."

"No, I mean it. Your friend really is here."

"Yeah? Which friend?"

"The woman you were with on New Year's Eve."

"Where?" That made the blood shoot to his dick, but it might not be Ellie. Alison had been at the club too.

"Sitting in the back near the bathroom." Paige put the lid on his drink.

His gaze landed on honey-brown hair and his feet followed. Her face was hidden behind a laptop but if it was Ellie, fate had decided that he didn't need to wait until Valentine's Day.

CHAPTER 26: ELLIE

Ellie stared at her laptop, trying to focus on the book she was reading but it was impossible with him in here stealing all the air. She refused to let herself look at him, but his image was etched into her mind. The blue jeans he wore hugged his delicious ass and the dark green T-shirt would make his eyes almost glow. She wanted to move closer to see those eyes but if she got anywhere near the man, she'd probably jump him. Dating mild non-alphas had proved to be not her thing.

She'd gone on two dates in the last few weeks and the men were kind, considerate and nice. They were everything she'd convinced herself that she wanted but there was no spark. She'd scoured the Internet on how to retrain her brain to be attracted to a different type of man, but it took time. Jumping alpha Adrian's bones would feel good but she wouldn't let herself. It'd be like an addict having another drink or snort, but it was so tempting.

She couldn't take it anymore. She had to steal one last glance. She shifted up in her seat, peeking over the top of her computer and her eyes landed on a pair of blue jeans and a bulge that she knew from personal experience could get much, much bigger. He was right there, across the table. Close enough to touch if she reached out her hand. All moisture fled from her throat and she croaked, "Adrian, what are you doing here? Stalking me?"

"Hardly, but how did you know it was me?"

She wanted to crawl under the table. Her eyes had never lifted from his crotch.

CHAPTER 27: ADRIAN

Adrian laughed. His day had gone from meh to fantastic because Ellie had definitely missed him if she could identify him by his dick, especially when it was concealed in his pants.

"I...I..." she stammered, sinking farther down in her chair.

"It's good to see you too."

"Ah...Thanks. Why are you here? You don't drink coffee."

"Neither do you."

"Yeah, but I live near here and..."

"Adrian, here's your tea." Paige tapped him on the shoulder and handed him his cup. "Nice to see you again." She smiled at Ellie before walking away.

"Sister's first day on the job." He held up his drink. "Thought I'd stop by for moral support."

"Oh, that's nice."

"Why are you hiding behind your laptop?" He started to pull out the chair across from her when Marc stormed into the store, shoving his way through the crowd.

"Damn it, Ellie. Where's the money?" Marc stopped at her table.

"Marc, calm down." Ellie stood.

"Don't tell me to fucking calm down. I could lose my business."

"Don't talk to her like that." Adrian stepped in front of Ellie.

"Who the fuck are you?" Marc shifted his stance, preparing for a fight. "Oh, you're the dick she fucked on Christmas Eve. Good for you. Now, get out of my way."

"No." Words were wasted on a guy like this. The only thing that worked was power.

"Adrian, this is between me and Marc," said Ellie

"I'm not going to let him talk to you like that."

"It's not your business," said Ellie.

His sister hurried over to them, tugging on his arm. "Adrian, let it go. The manager is going to call the cops."

"Listen to your sister." Ellie stepped around him.

He let his sister pull him aside but made sure he blocked the path to the door and was close enough to hear them. It'd take him two seconds or less to stop Marc if the guy became violent.

"Marc, you're not going to lose the business if you pay the bill," said Ellie.

"That bill was supposed to be paid already and now they're charging me a late fee."

"Supposed to be paid? By who? Me? We broke up. I told you I wasn't paying your bills."

"Right, because you're paying his now." Marc pointed

at Adrian. "You're such a fucking slut."

That was it. Adrian flew forward grabbing Marc's shoulder. The other man swung around as fast as a cat, his fist flying. Adrian braced for the punch when Paige slammed into his side, knocking him off balance. He wrapped his arms around her as they fell, crashing onto a table and then landing on the floor, his body protecting hers from the brunt of the fall.

"That's it." The manager and a few of the customers hurried between them. "I'm calling the cops. The two of you are going to want to get as far away from here as you can. Now." The manager helped Paige to her feet.

Adrian stood, his eyes never leaving Marc's. "This isn't over."

"Damn right, it's not."

"Adrian, let it go." Ellie pushed between them. "Go home."

"Listen to her pussy-boy or you're going get your ass handed to you." Marc walked toward the door.

The manager and a few of the bigger, male customers stayed between the two.

"And who's going to do that?" He taunted as he followed Marc. "It sure as fuck won't be some abusive cocksucker like you."

"Oh, yeah. I could take you out in two seconds but I ain't getting arrested over that bitch." Marc gave Ellie a disgusted look.

Adrian wanted to bury his fist down the guy's throat but instead said, "Then let's take this somewhere we won't get arrested. Unless you're too scared."

CHAPTER 28: ELLIE

"Don't. please." Ellie clung to Adrian's arm. "It's not worth it." She didn't want him to get hurt.

"Yeah, pussy." Marc stepped outside of the coffee shop, Adrian right behind him. "Listen to her. You don't want that pretty face messed up."

"Time and place. Name it."

"Adrian, don't." Ellie yanked on his arm but of course, he wasn't listening to her.

"My club—"

"No. It won't be a fair fight." She let go of Adrian. Marc was a professional fighter. Adrian wasn't.

"I would never cheat," said Marc.

Ellie was pretty sure her jaw hit the sidewalk. "*You* would never cheat?"

Marc had the decency to look embarrassed but then he ruined it by opening his mouth. "Fighting is important to me. I'd never cheat."

"Where and when?" Adrian's voice had taken on an icy quality that made Ellie shiver.

"Adrian, forget it." She took his hand. "Please. For

me."

He looked down at her, his face softening. "I'm doing this for you." He turned back to Marc. "Name it."

"My club. Now."

"Address."

"No." She tried to make Adrian look at her, but his focus was on Marc. "Don't do this."

"Gabe's Gym." Marc gave him the address. "It's about twenty minutes from here. You can't miss it. We'll meet in the ring in an hour." He got into his car and left.

Adrian pulled his phone from his pocket and started walking.

"Wait." She ran after him. It wasn't too late to change his mind. "Please, let it go."

"No." He pressed a button on his phone and raised it to his ear. "Mitch, I need you to meet me at Gabe's Gym in forty minutes or less. Grab my gym bag from my place. A fight. His yard. Nope. I'm at the coffee shop where my sister works. I don't have my car."

"Please don't do this." She hurried in front of him and stopped, making him stop. "It won't be a fair fight."

He didn't even look at her. "Yeah. I'll start walking. See you." He hung up his phone. "Ellie, get out of my way."

"Please, let's go talk. Have lunch. Something. Anything."

"It'll be fine. I have friends coming. It'll be alright." He stepped around her.

"How will that help?" Being surrounded by friends

when he got his ass whooped wasn't going to make things better. She followed him.

"They'll make sure he follows the rules."

"Marc won't break the rules." She tried not to wince. She shouldn't have said that.

He stopped. "But you said it wouldn't be a fair fight." He paused for a second. "Wait a minute. You're not worried about him cheating, are you?"

"Uh...yeah. Of course." She glanced away.

"You are such a liar." Usually his voice was filled with laughter and fondness when he called her that but this time it was laced with anger. "You think I can't win."

She bit the inside of her lower lip to keep from speaking. The truth would make him feel like he needed to prove himself and that wouldn't end well for him.

"Admit it. You think I'm going to get my ass kicked."

She stayed silent.

"Unfucking believable." He started walking again, but she blocked him.

"Adrian, please don't do this."

"I can hold my own." He stepped around her.

"I'm sure you can but this is stupid." She followed, blocking his path again.

"Not to me. I'd kick his ass if he said that to one of my sisters and I'm going to kick his ass for saying that to you." He grabbed her shoulders, lifted her, dropped her to the side and strode past.

"Wait." She hurried after him her stupid heart twisting with worry and something else that scared her even more.

CHAPTER 29: ADRIAN

"Ellie, go back to the coffee shop." Adrian couldn't wait to put his fist in Marc's face. He'd been wanting to do it since the day they'd met.

"Okay but only if you come with me. Please."

"After the fight." He continued walking.

"Damn it." She raced to keep up with him, grabbing his sleeve.

"Ellie, I'm doing this." He shook her hand free from his arm.

"You are such an ass."

That stopped him. He spun toward her. "Me? I'm the ass?"

"Yes." She slapped his arm. "I knew something like this was going to happen when I saw you come into the coffee shop."

"You saw me come…You were hiding from me?" That hurt worse than any punch he was going to get from Marc.

"Yes, but only because…"

He turned and walked away. He was such a fool. He

was going to beat the shit out of some guy for a woman who wanted nothing to do with him.

"Adrian, please wait." She hurried after him.

He walked faster. "Go away, Ellie and don't worry I won't bother you again."

"That's not...Please, let me explain."

Mitch's car pulled up to the curb.

"Did you bring my gym bag?" he asked as he hopped into the car.

"Yep. What's going on?"

"I'm going to beat the shit out of some asshole." He closed the door.

"Adrian, wait!" Ellie yelled as she hurried toward them.

"Who's that?" asked Mitch.

"Ellie."

"Should I wait?"

"Nope. Drive."

CHAPTER 30: ELLIE

By the time Ellie got to Gabe's Gym she was sweating, swearing and terrified. Marc had been furious when he'd seen the hickey on her neck. He'd never hit her, but he'd take great pleasure in taking out all his rage on Adrian. She shouldn't have gotten involved with Adrian until Marc was gone from her life. Now, he was going to get hurt and it was all her fault.

She burst into the building. A large crowd surrounded the ring. Adrian was already in there, dressed for the fight—no shirt and loose shorts. Marc stepped out of the locker room and headed toward the ring.

"Marc, wait." But he kept walking and disappeared in the crowd. She hurried across the gym. She had to stop this fight. She pushed past a couple of large guys. "Let me through. Please."

She could barely see anything but bodies, but she could hear Gabe telling them both the rules. The tightness around her chest eased a bit. Gabe would make sure Marc didn't keep beating Adrian once he was down.

"Please. Let me through. Please. I have to stop this."

The men and women barely moved out of her way, but it was enough for her to squeeze through. She finally pushed to the front. Marc and Adrian circled each other like predators looking for a weakness.

"Stop! Adrian! Listen to me!" He glanced at her and she screamed as Marc kicked him in the face.

CHAPTER 31: ADRIAN

Adrian staggered backward from the force of Marc's foot to his face.

"Damn it," yelled Mitch. "Pay attention to the fight."

Adrian blocked the next punch and backed away from Marc. Fuck, that'd hurt but Mitch was right. He tuned out Ellie's yells and the cheers from the crowd. Calm settled over him as everything disappeared except his opponent.

Marc seemed to feed on the excitement because the guy began to show off. He did a handstand and launched himself into a flip. Then he spun, kicking in the air. Marc was too far away to be of any danger, but it gave Adrian the time and opportunity to study his enemy. There was no doubt the guy had skills but that alone wouldn't win a fight.

Marc did a backflip, moving straight into a handstand before launching himself onto his feet, as gracefully as a cat. The guy was fast and agile. Adrian wasn't going to get too many shots, so he had to make the ones he did get count.

"Marc! Adrian! Stop. Gabe, please make them stop," begged Ellie.

"You should've thought about this before you fucked him, Ellie," said Marc. "You're a cheating whore."

Adrian was going to kill him. There was no reason to talk to her like that.

"Pay attention to the ring, fellas. Nothing else," said Gabe.

"Right. This will only take a minute." Marc moved toward Adrian, doing flips to cross the ring.

Adrian waited. The guy was sure to land close and position for a punch. That'd be the opening he needed. He shut out Ellie's screams, hearing nothing but the beat of his heart and the swoosh of his enemy approaching. Time seemed to slow as Marc moved closer. One more flip and Marc straightened, his fist flying toward Adrian's face. That was it. The guy was fast but wide open. Adrian ducked and dodged, stepping forward and landing a punch right on Marc's jaw. Marc hit the mat and the crowd fell silent.

Gabe walked over and bent down by Marc. "One. Two."

"Get up you bastard," Adrian yelled as Gabe kept counting. "I'm not done beating the shit out of you." But Marc didn't move.

"Six. Seven." Gabe continued to count.

"This is bullshit." His blood surged through him, ready to fight but it was over. Marc was out cold.

"Ten," shouted Gabe before walking toward Adrian.

Adrian raised his arms in victory and said to Gabe, "Tell the fucker to leave her alone." He nodded at Ellie.

"I don't get involved in his personal business," said Gabe.

"Then give him the message from me." He headed toward Mitch and his other friends, Sonny and Derek.

"That was fucking awesome." Mitch slapped his back and handed him his shirt. "Let's go celebrate."

"Adrian, Adrian," yelled Ellie as she tried to push her way through the crowd.

He pulled on his shirt and kept walking.

"Aren't you going to wait for her?" asked Mitch. "You just knocked a guy out for her."

"Nope." He walked faster. If he talked to her right now, he'd fuck her and although his body really wanted that his head didn't. She'd hid from him. From him.

"Okay." Mitch and the others followed him out of the building.

"Adrian. Stop. Damn you." Ellie chased them through the parking lot.

Mitch pressed the button on his key chain and opened his car.

"I need to go home and shower." He glanced at Sonny and Derek. "Drinks are on me tonight."

"Sure." Derek glanced back at Ellie. "If you don't make it tonight, drinks are on you tomorrow." He and Sonny headed for Derek's truck.

"I'll make it." He hollered as he hopped into the car and slammed the door.

"Adrian." Ellie stopped a few feet from the car her face pale and forlorn.

Mitch got into the driver's side. "Are you really going to leave her like this?"

"Yep." He couldn't talk to her right now.

"Okay." Mitch started the car and backed up. He'd just put it in drive when the first drop of rain hit the windshield, followed by another. The sky was about to open up and drown them all.

"Fuck. I can't win." Adrian wanted to put his fist through the window.

"You won the fight and now you get the prize," said Mitch but he didn't drive away. "She's just standing there staring at the car like a dumped dog. Do you think she'll chase after us when we drive off?" He chuckled.

"Shut the fuck up." No one said anything bad about Ellie around him, not even his best friend.

"Sorry." Mitch didn't sound sorry at all. "Do you want me to drive or what?"

"No. Tell her to hurry her ass up."

"It'd be better if you—"

"Just fucking do it. I'm not speaking to her."

"Okay." Mitch rolled down the window and yelled, "Adrian said to come on if you want a ride." He leaned back into the car, shaking the rain off his head. "Looks like she wants a ride you lucky bastard. Drinks tomorrow on you."

"Nope. Tonight. You're taking me home and then you can take her wherever she wants to go."

"Right." Mitch laughed. "Like that's going to happen."

CHAPTER 32: ELLIE

Ellie hopped into the back seat of Adrian's friend's car. Her hair and shirt already soaked from the downpour.

"Hi, I'm Mitch," said the driver. He was good looking, muscular with blonde hair and brown eyes.

"I'm Ellie. Thank you for stopping." She was pretty sure it hadn't been Adrian's idea. He was pissed at her, again.

"It was his decision." Mitch tipped his head at Adrian and then pulled out onto the road.

"Oh."

"Wow, you sound surprised." Mitch glanced at Adrian.

"No. Not really. I mean, I am but only because I know he's mad at me." She leaned forward toward Adrian. "Oh, your poor face." A bruise was already forming on his cheek and there was a large gash under his eye. She touched right below his cut. "You need something cold on that and the cut needs to be clea—"

"It's fine." He turned away from her.

She dropped her hand and leaned against the back seat. He was pissed and she didn't blame him. He'd been hurt because of her. She should apologize but it was clear he didn't want to talk to her right now. She stared out the window, watching the storm but all she saw was Adrian getting kicked in the face.

"Seems like the storm is passing," said Mitch. "Fast and furious, just like your fists."

Adrian grunted an answer.

"Okay then. How about some music?" Mitch turned on the radio.

It filled the silence but did nothing to eliminate the awkwardness. She had to apologize. She leaned forward again. "I'm sorry I yelled, and that you got kicked in the face."

"Forget it."

"I can't forget it." Seeing his head snap to the side was carved into her memory like a scar. She couldn't even imagine how badly that must've hurt and it was all her fault.

Mitch pulled into the parking lot at Adrian's apartment complex and stopped the car in front the building.

"Then remember it forever"—Adrian got out of the car—"because I don't give a shit what you do." He looked at his friend. "I'll see you at Marley's in an hour." He slammed the door.

Adrian's words hit her like a punch. He was more than angry; he was furious with her. She had to talk to him. "Wait."

She started to get out, but he grabbed the top of her door, stopping her from opening it any wider.

"Mitch is taking you home."

"We need to talk." She wasn't going to be sent away like a naughty child.

"No, we don't." He leaned down by the crack. "Mitch as soon as I close this door, drive."

"Don't you dare." She shoved at the door, but Adrian wasn't budging. "You can't force me to stay in this car." She shoved again. "Let me out."

"Adrian, people are starting to stare." Mitch pointed at the two women taking groceries out of their car. "I don't feel like getting arrested for kidnapping."

"Fine." Adrian looked at her. "Go home."

"I'm not going home."

"Then go back to the coffee shop."

"No. We—"

"Then go any place you fucking want except here." He let go and strode up the stairs to his apartment.

She pushed the door open all the way.

"Don't do it, Ellie," warned Mitch. "Let me take you home."

"I need to talk to him." She had to apologize and to thank him for sticking up for her.

"If you're not serious about him, let him go."

"Serious?" That stopped her. She stared at Mitch. "I just need to talk to him."

"Uh-huh."

"Really. That's it and then I'm going home." Even she wasn't so sure about that. She hated fighting but seeing him in the ring—calm and focused, not showing off while Marc played the crowd—had made her body turn molten. The fact that he hadn't been wearing his shirt hadn't hurt either but when he'd been kicked in the face, she'd felt that blow to her stomach and her heart. Then, when he'd taken Marc down with one punch, she'd wanted nothing more than to jump him, kiss him, and take care of him in every way she could.

CHAPTER 33: ADRIAN

"Son of a bitch," Adrian almost shouted when he heard the knock. "Fuck this." He turned off the shower and strode to the door, flinging it open. "Go away."

Ellie stood with her arm raised to knock again. Her cheeks were flushed, and her hair messed. Except for being soaked from the rain, she looked like she did right after he'd fucked her, and his dick wanted that again.

"Oh, your face." She winced. "It looks worse in the light." She touched his cheek. "I'm sorry about this. We need to clean—"

He jerked his head away. "Ellie, go home." His voice was calm, but it was a mask because his blood surged through his body, primal from the adrenaline. He'd fought. He'd won. He'd defended her honor. She belonged to him.

"I'm not going home. We need—"

"Then go somewhere else." If she didn't leave soon, he'd pull her into his apartment and fuck her.

"Not until we talk." She stared up at him. "May I come in?"

"That depends." He stepped closer, letting her feel how

much bigger he was than her, how much stronger.

"On what?" Her eyes moved across his bare chest and then back up to his face.

"On why you want to come in."

"To talk." She frowned. "To apologize. This was—"

"Then no."

"What? But I want to apologize for—"

"I don't want your apology." He didn't want words at all. Moans, grunts and the sound of rough sex was all he wanted to hear.

"Too bad because you're going to get it." She tried to push under his arm, but he caught her shoulder.

"Ellie, if you step into this apartment, we're not going to talk."

She stared up at him, her brown eyes huge. He had to make sure she understood because with the way he was feeling right now, once she was inside, he wouldn't be able to stop himself from taking what he'd won.

"I want to make this clear. If you put one foot inside my place, I'm going to fuck you. It's not going to be gentle. It's going to be what I want. How I want it and how ever many times as I want it. Understand?"

"Perfectly." Her eyes narrowed.

He moved aside. She stood frozen, staring past him into the apartment like it was a fucking cave or something. He was so done with all of her bullshit but his cock wasn't done. It still wanted her. His blood roared for her.

"Tick-tock. You need to make up your mind. I have plans tonight." He leaned against the side of the doorframe.

"I'm counting to three and shutting the door. One."

"I want to talk. That's all."

"Two."

"Promise me that if I come inside, we'll—"

"I told you what'll happen if you step inside this apartment and I wasn't kidding. At all."

"Adrian, come on."

"Three." He slammed the door.

CHAPTER 34: ELLIE

Ellie stared at the door to Adrian's apartment. He'd shut it in her face. Not just shut it, he'd slammed it. He was the rudest man she'd ever met. Oh, he was so going to get a piece of her mind. She grabbed the doorknob and flung the door open, stepping inside. "Don't you ever…"

He was already halfway to his bedroom but he stopped, spun around and in two seconds he was in front of her, his mouth covering hers, his hands on her ass, pulling her against him and all she could do was soften into his hardness.

Without thought her arms wrapped around his neck, clinging to him as he pushed the door shut and shoved her against it. His hands were everywhere at once. He lifted her shirt and bra, his hot mouth covering her breast as he rubbed between her legs. She moaned, opening wider for his touch. She'd needed this, wanted this. He pulled her forward and swatted her ass.

"Hey, that hu…" Her words turned into a moan as he pinched her nipple. Sensations of pain, pleasure, need and desire zipped through her body as his hands squeezed, caressed and teased her everywhere.

"You drive me fucking mad." He swatted her ass again.

"Hey, I don't…"

His mouth covered hers, stopping her protest as his hand slid into her pants. She groaned as he stroked her, his fingers rough on her tender flesh. He unbuttoned her jeans, shoving them down and then he was on his knees spreading her legs. She gasped as he buried his face in her pussy, licking and sucking. His fingers dug into her thighs and his tongue slid between her slick folds before dipping inside her. She arched into his face. Her fingers clung to his hair, keeping him in place. His hands moved to her ass, lifting her like an offering as he fed on her swollen flesh. His tongue alternated between sliding deep inside her, filling her and retreating to lap at her folds before teasing her clit. Her legs trembled as his lips covered her clit and he sucked. A jolt of pain-pleasure shot though her. She screamed, pushing him away but he held her still as he increased his assault, sucking harder and sliding two fingers inside her, pumping fast.

"Oh…god…Adrian. I can't…oh…oh…oh!" Her body tightened. He added another finger, stretching her while his tongue teased her clit. His fingers curled, hitting her G-spot and she screamed as she shattered.

He stood, wincing slightly as he wiped his mouth with the back of his hand before kissing her and letting her taste herself on him. He pulled away and grabbed her chin, his face hard with passion or anger. She wasn't sure which.

"Do not move. At all. Got it?"

She nodded because she was pretty sure she'd collapse into a boneless puddle of mush if she tried.

CHAPTER 35: ADRIAN

Adrian had been preparing for this since New Year's Eve. He'd stashed condoms all around his apartment and now he congratulated himself on his forethought.

He took two steps to the TV stand and grabbed a condom from a small drawer. He turned back around, expecting Ellie to be ready to talk or argue but she was still leaning against the door, her pants down around her feet and her pussy waiting for him, dripping for him.

He must've made some kind of noise because her eyes met his. They were soft and dazed from her orgasm and he was going to give her another one. He pushed his shorts and underwear down, kicking them away as he tore the condom open and walked toward her.

Her gaze dropped to his erection. His cock and his pride grew at the slight widening of her eyes. Yes, it was all for her and he was going to give it to her good.

He stopped in front of her, sliding the condom over his dick before grabbing her chin. Her gaze was still slightly unfocused but her mouth...Those lips were lush and red, swollen from his kisses. Just like her pussy. Swollen. Wet.

Needy for him. He ran his dick through her slit as he kissed her, not even feeling the pain from the kick to his face as his tongue explored her mouth. He let go of her chin, kissing her stomach as he bent and pulled her shoes and pants off, tossing them aside. He stood, lifting her leg to his hip while his other hand positioned his cock at her entrance. He kept his lips on hers, needing to feel her gasp when he made her body surrender to his. He thrust into her in one hard push and she gasped against his lips.

That was all it took. He'd already been on edge, needing to fuck after the fight. He raised her other leg to his waist. She had nothing grounding her except him and the door. She clung to him, her breath coming in short, hot pants against his mouth as he plunged into her again and again. Today he had no finesse, no style. He fucked hard and fast and she responded. Her body squeezed him while little moans of pleasure escaped her lips and filled his soul as he made her his.

He grabbed her hair, pulling his mouth away from hers as he yanked back her head. "Look at me." He needed her to see that it was him giving her this pleasure. Him. No one else made her feel this way. No one else made her come twice. He needed to see her release, see those brown eyes sharpened with pleasure and then drift away with her orgasm.

Her eyes fluttered open and locked with his. He twisted her hair in his hand, holding her in place. Her eyes darkened with each thrust, pleading with him, and hopefully, seeing him, really seeing *him* for the first time.

Her moans came faster, and her nails dug into his back, the pain driving him on. Her body squeezed his, tugging him deeper and deeper until his thrusts were nothing more than short, hard jabs.

"Oh…oh….god." Her eyes drifted shut as her body started to shake.

"Look at me." He yanked on her hair and her eyes opened, meeting his again. She moaned, long and low. Her body clasped onto his like a vise as her hips bucked, milking his dick. He fucked her faster now, riding her movement as her climax shoved him over the edge. His lips found hers and he gasped into her mouth as he came.

CHAPTER 36: ELLIE

Ellie woke, stretching. She felt wonderful. Even the soreness between her legs felt good—like the ache of muscles after a workout and she'd definitely had a good workout.

After the episode at the door, Adrian had carried her to his bed and had proceed to fuck her again. She had no idea how he'd managed but the man was insatiable, and it was glorious. She'd missed wild sex. Her happiness slipped a notch. Sex was always like this at the beginning. Alpha males were great in bed, but they sucked at everything else that was needed in a relationship.

She should've never walked into this apartment. Her body didn't regret it, but her head did. She was spiraling right into another heartache. She was starting to really like Adrian and that'd be the beginning of the end. Men like him loved the chase, fed off it, but once they captured their target their interest waned and so did the sex.

She sat up and looked around the room. The house was quiet, but she was sure he was lurking around here somewhere. Not that she'd take the coward's way out and sneak away, but she wasn't looking forward to seeing him. He'd be funny and sexy and charming, and she needed to get out of there before she became even more involved.

Her eyes landed on her clothes which lay neatly folded on a chair and her damn heart swelled like it was infected. That was it. Adrian was an infection just like all the other alphas she'd dated but none of them had ever done something like this. They'd either liked seeing her parade around naked while looking for her clothes, or they hadn't given her comfort a second thought which was probably closer to the truth. Wolves didn't worry about the deer after they'd fed.

She got out of bed and picked up her shirt. It was dry-completely dry like he'd tossed it into the dryer. Her heart stuttered again. Maybe Adrian was different—sexy and alpha but different. She pulled on her clothes and went into his bathroom. Could she have it all? A man she was attracted to—more than attracted, ravenous for—and who'd care for her enough to stay faithful. Was that even possible? She splashed water on her face. She was a mess—her hair in tangles, her lips red and her cheeks flushed. She looked like she'd been fucked brainless which she had. She used his brush to straighten her hair the best she could. The rain and his fingers, not to mention the door and the bed, had made her hair uncontrollable. The only real fix was a shower and as much as she wanted to soak in some hot water, she wasn't getting naked in this house again. She needed to go home, get Marc out of her apartment and then think about what she was going to do about Adrian. Her head told her to move on, but her body said to jump him and take this ride as far as it went.

She brushed her teeth with toothpaste and her finger and then left the bathroom. The bedroom was still empty, so she walked into the living room. He was sitting on the couch, his phone in his hand.

He looked up at her. "Hey." His green eyes sparkled like they shared a secret which they did—the secret of fabulous sex.

"Hey." Until him, she'd never done this one-night stand kind of thing, although after three times she could hardly call it one night, but it was still awkward. Probably because she'd been raised to believe that casual sex wasn't the thing to do and this was casual. It had to be. She wasn't ready to be involved with someone so soon after her last fiasco.

"You hungry? I'm starving." A mostly empty bag of potato chips sat on the table next to him. "I thought we could go out and grab something." He smiled, that sexy smirk that made her body melt. "I'd planned on meeting Mitch for lunch after I saw my sister but…" He stood, walking toward her like a panther after a fawn who didn't have the sense to run. "Fate had other ideas."

She didn't move. She should but…it'd been so good, and he'd fought for her. The bruise on his cheek and his slightly swollen eye reminding her that he'd gone to battle for her. He'd risked himself because of her. It didn't matter that the world believed fighting was bad, arrogance was bad, alpha males were toxic, she melted at the thought of a man she could completely trust, one who she could count on in the worst situations.

He gently ran his hand over her cheek and bent, kissing her softly. "Or we could order take out and go back to bed."

Oh god, she wanted that. Her body throbbed for his, but she had to go. She couldn't do this again but instead of disagreeing like she'd planned, she said, "That'd be nice."

CHAPTER 37: ADRIAN

A soft sound, like someone trying to be quiet, woke Adrian. He was exhausted but in the best way. His balls were empty and his belly full. After Ellie had woke that afternoon, he'd expected her to run for the door as usual but instead they'd fucked and ordered pizza and then fucked again. His day may have started out normal and then turned to crap, but it was ending as the best day he'd had in a long time, maybe ever. He had every intention of finishing the rest of it on a high note. The only problem with that was the woman who was the reason for every up and down he'd had today was quietly getting dressed.

"Where do you think you're going."

She jumped and he laughed as he sat up, leaning against the headboard.

"It's not funny. You scared me." She stepped into her jeans.

"Good because you're scaring me. Why are you getting dressed?" He pulled back the covers. "Get back in bed."

"I can't." She fastened her bra and grabbed her shirt.

"You can." He had to convince her to stay. "Are you hungry? How about Chinese food for dinner?"

She smiled blushing a bit. "I shouldn't have stayed for lunch." She put her foot on the bed and pulled on her sock. "I have to get home."

"Why?" He scooted across the bed. "Stay. I'll take you home tomorrow."

She turned, giving him a quick kiss on the side of his mouth. That was not a good sign.

"I can't." She touched his cheek, her fingers drifting softly near the bruise. "I'm so sorry I got you messed up in this."

"I won with one punch." He'd be telling his grandkids about that fight.

"I know. It was awesome." She kissed him again and even though she didn't miss his mouth this time, the kiss was too fast and not at all intimate.

"It was. I can't wait to do it again." He grinned.

"No more fighting, but I can't help wishing that I'd recorded it." She smiled and then her eyes grew serious. "But I do have to go. Thank you.'"

Shit. She was getting ready for her thanks but no thanks speech, but it wasn't going to happen this time. He grabbed her hand. "Why? It's Saturday. You don't have to work tomorrow. I don't have to work."

"I need to shower."

"You can shower here." His grin widened. "We can shower together. You know, conserve water."

She laughed. "I don't think that's a good idea.

"But it is." He inched closer. "It's an excellent idea and it's good for the environment."

"The environment will have to deal with us taking separate showers like we have been all our lives." She pulled her hand from his. "Seriously, I have to go."

"Okay. I'll drive you." He got out of bed, grabbing his clothes. He had the ride to her house to change her mind.

"You don't have to do that."

"I want to."

"No. I can take an—"

"I said I'd drive you." Maybe he could convince her to stop for dinner and that might lead to drinks which could lead back to his bed.

"Okay. Thanks." She didn't look like she was sure about this, but he had every intention of changing her mind.

CHAPTER 38: ADRIAN

The ride to Ellie's apartment was quiet, quieter than Adrian would've liked but sometimes women needed space. He'd seen his older sisters like this. When they'd been younger, they'd been thrilled and super excited about any new guy they'd dated but as time went by that excitement had been replace by doubt and hesitation. The guys who made it though, the ones who won the game, were the ones who didn't push. It went against every instinct he had but he'd give her some space and some time but not much. He wanted her in his life and his bed, and he was going to do whatever he had to do to get that.

He parked his car in an empty space next to her building.

"Thanks. I'm glad I got to see you knock Marc out." She smiled and his heart basically disintegrated.

Her smiles were always gorgeous but this one could be used as a weapon. It was devastating in its honesty. It was a smile that'd last a lifetime. Every time she remembered him knocking out Marc, she'd smile like this—even if it were only in her head—and then she'd remember him. It was the most arousing thing he'd ever experienced.

"Anytime." He smiled. "I mean that. Seriously." He'd love to beat the guy on a daily basis.

She laughed and got out of the car. He followed. She stopped, staring at him over the roof. It was deja vu, and it was pissing him off.

"It's daylight. I'm safe going to my apartment by myself."

"People get attacked and kidnapped during the day too."

"I'm fine."

"I'll walk you to the door." He was getting really tired of this argument.

"Please don't take this the wrong way but I'd rather you didn't."

"I only see one way to take that."

"It's just that….I know you can hold your own with Marc but—"

"He's still living here?" This was beyond anything he'd ever fucking imagined.

"Yeah, he's looking for a place but—"

"It's been almost a month."

"Three weeks."

"It doesn't matter. It's too long. Why in the hell is he still here?"

"He hasn't found anything yet."

"So what? I'm sure there are plenty of people at Gabe's that'd let him crash at their place. He seemed to have a following." Of course, today probably drastically reduced Marc's fan club and Adrian couldn't be happier.

"I don't want to argue about this."

"Good. Then let's not argue."

"Thank you again for taking me home."

"I'm walking you to your apartment." It was typical of a female to think that not arguing meant she'd won.

"Please don't."

He gave her a look that made it clear he really didn't care what she wanted.

"Fine." She turned and walked into the building.

He followed her, neither of them saying a word as they walked through the foyer and got into the elevator. He didn't want it to end like the other time. "Look, I'm not thrilled with him living here but I trust you."

"You trust me?" She was obviously taking this the wrong way.

"Yeah. I know the two of you aren't together." He didn't know shit, but he was pretty sure she wouldn't have run to him to make sure he was all right while her boyfriend was knocked out on the mat. "I know you have things you need to deal with, but I'd like to see you." At her frown he added. "It can be lunch, dinner, coffee, not-coffee." He smiled.

"I don't think that's a good idea."

The elevator stopped and they walked toward her apartment.

"Why?" He was a former Marine. He did not give up that easily.

"Because"—she lowered her voice—"we end up in

bed every time we meet."

"That's why we should meet more often."

"No." But she smiled. His charm was working its magic. She touched his cheek, her fingers drifting lightly over his bruise. "Thank you but I still need time."

"How much?" He was being too pushy, but he couldn't help it.

"I'll call you."

"Will you? Don't say it if you don't mean it." He'd heard his sisters use that line and he'd even heard his brother-in-law throw it back at his sister when they'd been dating. At the time he'd classified the guy as a wuss but now he recognized the brilliance behind the words. Women hated it when men said that and didn't call, so they'd make sure they did call.

"I...I....Okay. You're right. I need to be honest and right now, I'm not sure about this. About us. About anything."

Wait a minute. That wasn't how it'd worked for his brother-in-law. "What do you mean?"

"Give me some time."

"How am I supposed to do that when you won't tell me how much and you won't agree to call me."

"I don't know how much, and I don't want to lie to you."

"You know what? That's cool. Goodbye." He strode toward the elevator, waiting for her to tell him to stop but all he heard was her opening her door. If that was what she wanted, it was fine with him. He didn't need her constant hot-cold routine anyway. He punched the button. The elevator couldn't get here soon enough but then he heard it—a gasp but not one of passion. It was the sound a woman made when she didn't want to cry. One that screamed that her heart had just been crushed and her world destroyed, and one that he damn well couldn't ignore.

CHAPTER 39: ELLIE

Ellie stared into her apartment. It was a complete disaster. Marc must've been furious when he'd gotten home. He'd unpacked everything of his that she'd spent days putting into boxes but worse than that, her things were thrown in piles on the floor. She couldn't stop her gasp when she saw the broken clock. It was all she had left from her great grandmother and it looked like Marc had put his foot through it. She walked over to it and bent, picking up the pieces but it was broken beyond repair.

"Ellie, what's wro…" Adrian stood in the doorway. "Tell me again why this asshole is still living here."

"He isn't starting today." She wiped her eyes and stormed out of the apartment.

"Where are you going?" Adrian followed her to the elevator.

"To talk to the landlady about kicking his ass out."

The elevator opened and a short, rotund woman with grayish-brown hair stepped into the hallway. "Ellie, I thought that was you in the lobby."

"Mrs. Carthouse, I was just coming to see you. I want

Marc out. He destroyed—"

"Oh dear." The woman seemed flustered.

"What's wrong?" Ellie's stomach tightened.

"Marc signed the papers today."

"He can't. He doesn't have any money. You told me that I'd have to give you first and last month's rent in advance because this was considered a new lease if Marc's name wasn't on it."

"Those aren't my rules but yes, it's what the owner wants."

"And Marc doesn't have that kind of money."

"He paid, dear. He paid six months up front. I couldn't turn that down. Mr. Vicky would fire me."

"He paid? How?"

Mrs. Carthouse took Ellie's hand. "I'm sorry dear but he had another woman with him."

"Another…" She shook her head. He'd found another wallet. That'd been all she was to him—a way to pay his bills. She swallowed down the hatred and anger over so much time wasted on that guy.

"I'm so sorry." Mrs. Carthouse patted her hand. "You're better off if you ask me."

"I know, I am." She was glad she'd discovered what kind of man he was before she'd married him.

"And I'm sure you'll have no problem finding another place to live"—Mrs. Carthouse's gaze landed on Adrian—"or another boyfriend."

"Him? No. We're just friends." The words were automatic, and she wanted to yank them out of the air and stuff them back inside her mouth, but it was too late. Adrian stiffened at her side, but she couldn't worry about his hurt feelings. "I guess I'd better start packing." She had no idea how she'd get it all done by Monday.

"Wait." Adrian spoke for the first time. "In this state the landlord has to give notice if they aren't renewing the lease."

"She's had thirty days, sir." Mrs. Carthouse straightened, her lips thinning.

"Thirty days? What is she talking about?" He looked at Ellie.

"Our lease was up the middle of December. We'd been talking about maybe buying a house. Mrs. Carthouse was kind enough to let us pay monthly until we decided what we were going to do." She'd been pushing Marc to take their relationship to the next level. She'd had no idea that their next level would be breaking up.

"So, why didn't you kick him out after Christmas Eve?"

"Because our names were both on the monthly lease which ends this week." Ellie had never thought Marc would do this. Not that he wasn't enough of a jerk but because he didn't have the money.

"When this week?" asked Adrian.

"It's up on Monday."

"Ah…no, that can't be right. It's up today," said Mrs. Carthouse.

"No. Monday," said Ellie.

"But I rented it to Marc, starting today." Mrs.

140

Carthouse's hands fluttered by her sides. "I hope I didn't mess this up. Mr. Vicky will be upset."

"There's no reason to involve Mr. Vicky." Ellie took the older woman's hand. "Since Marc and I aren't on speaking terms, just let him know that I have through Sunday to move my things."

"He's not going to be happy, dear."

"That makes two of us." She nodded and forced herself to smile. She had no idea how she was going to get everything moved by then or where she'd go.

"What if he won't agree?" Mrs. Carthouse's face was flushed with worry. "I need this job."

"Just talk to him. Marc likes you and if I have to, I'll talk to him too. Mr. Vicky doesn't need to hear anything about this."

"Thank you, dear." Mrs. Carthouse stepped inside the elevator.

Ellie walked back to her apartment, Adrian at her side.

"That was nice of you," he said.

"She's a nice lady. Her husband died and she needs the job."

"Still, she fucked up." He followed her into her apartment.

"Taking out my frustration on her won't make my problems go away." And she had a ton of problems. She had to pack all her stuff, move it, and find somewhere to store it. Then she had to find a place to live.

"That's true. Tell me where to start."

"Why are you helping me?" She'd just told him she

didn't want to see him anymore and yet, here he was offering to help her move. A task no one wanted to do. It made her want to cry, hug him and hide from him at the same time.

"There's no way you're moving all this in a little more than a day by yourself"—he frowned—"or just with my help." He pulled his phone from his pocket. "I can call some friends, but it'll cost you beer and pizza."

She wanted to fling herself into his arms but instead she nodded, afraid her voice would crack if she spoke.

"I'll make the call." He walked into the hallway.

She picked up her purse by the door and took out her phone. With his help she might get things moved but she had nowhere to take everything and nowhere to live. She called Alison. That should take care of the living part which left finding a storage facility.

CHAPTER 40: ELLIE

Ellie directed Adrian and his friends to start packing the boxes into the truck she'd rented. She still had no idea where she'd put the stuff once the vehicle was loaded. Every storage facility that she'd called had either been full or closed for the weekend.

"Ellie!" Alison rushed into the apartment and hugged her. "Marc is such an ass."

"I won't argue with that." Ellie headed for her bedroom where she'd been packing her clothes and Alison followed.

She still had to ask her friend if she could stay with her for a few days. She'd tried to explain everything over the phone, but as soon as Alison had heard that Marc had signed the lease and Ellie needed to move, her friend had hung up and rushed over.

She grabbed another armful of clothes from the closet. "Thanks for coming. I need to ask a favor."

"Sure. Anything." Alison pointed at the dresser. "You need this packed too?"

"No. Adrian said they can move it as is and I can

empty it later."

"Later? What if you need the clothes?" asked Alison.

"We don't have time. I have to be out tomorrow, remember?" That was one of the few things she'd told her friend before Alison had hung up.

"Right. I noticed that Adrian's here." Alison's voice took on a teasing tone.

"It's not like that." She wasn't going to explain what it was like because she still didn't understand it herself.

"Right, because everyone likes to help people move for free."

"I'm buying them beer and pizza."

"Oh, that explains it." Alison grabbed another box and started helping Ellie empty the closet.

"It doesn't and I know that, but I can't think about Adrian right now. I don't even know where I'm going to go." She turned to her friend. "Here comes the favor. Can I stay with you and your mom for a while?"

"Uhm…" Alison's hand froze around a group of hangars.

Ellie stopped. She hadn't even considered that this would be a problem. "It won't be long. Only until I find a place."

"Sure. Of course. It's just that Aunt Tiff is still in town."

"I thought she went home after New Year's Day."

"She does…usually, but this year she decided to stay longer."

"Oh. Okay. No problem. I'll stay at a hotel." That was

going to cost a fortune because it'd be a least a few days before she found a place to rent.

"The sublet on my apartment is up in two weeks. I can tell her that she needs to move. I can even ask her if she can move out earlier."

"No. She's nice. Don't do that to her."

"Are you sure?"

"Yeah." She wasn't but that poor woman shouldn't have to upturn her life because Ellie dated assholes.

"I found you a place to store your stuff." Harker walked into the room with Adrian right behind him.

"How did…" She looked at Alison. Her eyes screaming, why is Harker here?

"I was working when you called. That's why I had to hang up." Alison sent Harker a disgusted look. "I had to get permission to leave…on a Saturday…evening."

"You're well compensated for your time,' said Harker.

"Not well enough," mumbled Alison.

She kept telling her friend that the man had the hots for her, but Alison refused to believe her. Unfortunately, she didn't have time to get into that now. "Thank you, Harker." Ellie grabbed her purse. "Do they have an online account, or should I write a check? How much is it?"

"It's free," said Harker.

"Free?" She looked up from digging for her credit card and checkbook.

"A friend of mine has a couple of empty buildings. He agreed to let you store your stuff in one of them."

"For how long?" She was grateful but she didn't trust

free.

Harker shrugged. "Ethan said for however long you need. He's not using the building and doesn't have any plans for it, at least not now."

"He owns an empty building?" It seemed like a waste of an investment. "I'll need to talk to him. Thank him and pay him something." She didn't like taking anything for free.

"Ellie, the truck is full. We need to get moving. Talk to him later, okay?" said Adrian.

"I don't know. What if he sells my things or—"

Harker laughed. "Ethan St. Johns doesn't need the few hundred dollars he'd get from selling your used furniture."

"Ethan St. Johns? From...the Club?" Adrian's tone was shocked.

Harker nodded. "The one and only."

"Don't worry about your stuff, Ellie. Harker's right. Ethan doesn't need to steal anything, and he wouldn't anyway."

"Ethan." She remembered that name. "Is that the gorgeous guy who owns La Petite Mort Club?"

"Yeah, but he's not that good looking." Adrian frowned.

Alison snorted. "If you say so. I've seen pictures. Trust me; he's been the star of many of my late-night fantasies."

Harker's eyes narrowed. "Adrian, are you ready to take a load to the facility because I'm more than ready to get out of here?"

"Yeah, but give me one minute," said Adrian.

Harker sent Alison one final glare and then left.

"What's his problem?" Alison glanced at Adrian and then Ellie. "Oh…you two want to….I'll go and help him." She scurried after Harker.

"Ellie." Adrian moved over by her. "I was coming to talk to you about the truck and I heard what Alison said about her house."

"Yeah." She made a face. "I'd thought for sure I could stay there but it's fine. I'll stay at a hotel until I find a place."

"That's silly." He brushed a strand of hair off her shoulder. "You can stay with me."

"I can't ask you to do that." Her heart started racing. She couldn't ask herself to do that.

"You didn't and it's not forever, just tonight or a couple of days. Whatever it takes until you to find a place."

"Adrian, that's sweet but—"

"Don't answer yet. Think about it." He bent and kissed her quickly. "You can tell me later after we're done here." He turned and left.

She stared after him. No matter how much she wanted to, she couldn't move in with him. Her heart wasn't ready to be broken again.

CHAPTER 41: ADRIAN

One more truck load and they'd be done moving Ellie's stuff to the storage facility. Adrian was hungry, sweaty and looking forward to tonight. He couldn't wait to spend time with Ellie—in and out of the bed. He wanted to get to know her better and a few days living together would do that.

He stepped off the elevator. Raised voices trickled down the hall. Marc was back. He ran toward the apartment.

"Don't do anything stupid," said Mitch as he and the other guys followed him.

"I bought that couch," yelled Marc.

"With my money, so that makes it mine," said Ellie.

Adrian burst into the apartment. If Marc was even close to Ellie, he'd beat the shit out of him.

Marc spun toward the door. "You fucker. Get out of my apartment."

"Make me." He stepped forward. "I'll be more than happy to kick your ass again."

"Marc. Adrian. Stop." Ellie moved between them.

"You were lucky but that won't happen twice," said Marc.

"Let's fight and see." He picked up Ellie and moved her out of his way.

"Do something. Stop them," Alison tugged on Harker's arm.

"Why? Let them settle it." Harker leaned against the kitchen counter.

"Stop it. Both of you." Ellie pushed between them again.

"Move the couch." Adrian glanced at Mitch. "We need room."

"Don't you dare," said Ellie.

Mitch and Sonny ignored her and picked up the couch, heading for the door.

"Put that down," said Marc. "It's mine."

"It is not." Ellie took a deep breath and stepped in front of Marc. "You can have the couch if you leave. Go. Come back tomorrow."

"I'm not leaving and it's my couch."

"I'm calling my lawyer," said a skinny, older woman.

"Who's that?" asked Adrian, but when Ellie ignored him, he looked at Alison.

"Marc's new girl...roommate."

"Oh." Marc had definitely not traded up. She'd probably been beautiful once but too much plastic surgery had made her look fake.

"I'm going to have you all arrested if you don't get out of here now." The woman pressed a button on her phone.

"Arrested? I don't think so but go ahead. Call the cops and your lawyer." He moved toward her. "This is Ellie's apartment until Monday."

"We signed the lease today," snapped the woman. "It's our place and we want you out."

"I paid for a month. My month is up Monday," said Ellie.

"Shit," said Marc.

The woman hung up the phone. "Is that true?"

"Yeah, baby. I forgot. I didn't think the slut would be home."

"Don't call her that. Ever." Adrian was going to kill the guy. He took one step, but Mitch blocked him.

"Or what?" Marc moved forward, his chest bumping Mitch's back.

"Marc, I'm asking you nicely to leave." Ellie voice was soft, but it cut through everything else. "This is my place until Monday."

"Our place. I'm on that lease too."

"Yes, it is but if you don't leave now, I'm calling a lawyer. I paid for almost everything you own. Your clothes, your workout equipment and even your business. If you don't leave now the lawyers can decide what part of all that actually belongs to me."

Adrian wasn't sure if he was impressed or scared by Ellie's ice queen routine.

"You can't do that," said Marc.

"Try me." She didn't even blink. "But if you leave now, I won't touch your personal stuff or your business."

Marc's jaw tightened.

"And I'll leave the couch."

"Let's go." Marc held out his hand to his new girlfriend before striding out of the apartment.

Adrian followed them into the hallway, hoping for a reason to kick Marc's ass again. Unfortunately, the two got into the elevator without looking back.

Ellie had finally done it. She'd gotten rid of Marc. No matter what she'd said, he'd had doubts about her true feelings for the asshole but, it was obviously over and that meant nothing stood in his way.

"Where is she?" He walked back into the apartment where Mitch and Derek were, none too gently, tipping the couch upside down in a corner.

"Bedroom," said Mitch.

That was the perfect room but too bad it wasn't his bedroom. He could use some alone time with her right now. He stepped into the doorway. Ellie and Alison were sitting on the bed.

"It's stupid to rent a hotel. Stay with him," said Alison.

"I can't. I won't make the same mistake again," said Ellie. "You saw what they're like when it ends. I'm not getting involved with someone like that again."

Adrian couldn't name the emotions that roared through him—anger, hurt, disappointment. They were all there and more, surging through his head.

"Ah...oh..." Alison stared up at him.

"Adrian," Ellie's voice was soft and surprised.

"Don't worry. I don't want to be in a relationship with

you either. I was offering a room to a friend." It was the biggest lie he'd ever told.

"What?" She blinked at him, a tear dropping from her long lashes onto her cheek. She looked sadder than the first day he'd seen her, but he had to stay strong, save some semblance of his pride.

"You thought I wanted you to move in with me like a girlfriend?" He forced himself to chuckle. "Sorry. No. I thought we'd made that all clear earlier. I was offering the spare room for tonight and maybe tomorrow. That's all."

"Oh...ah...I don't..."

"Whatever. We've got one more load to take and then I'm out of here. You can stay at my place or not. Makes no difference to me." He lied again because right now, he didn't want her anywhere near him.

CHAPTER 42: ELLIE

"Ellie, are you okay?" asked Alison

"Yeah. Sure." She sat at the table in Murphy's with her friend. The guys, including Adrian, were at the bar. Even Harker had joined them to play pool.

They laughed and joked and flirted with the waitresses. The bartender seemed to save her flirting for Adrian. All Ellie wanted to do was go home but she had no home.

"You can stay with me. I'll take the couch," said Alison.

"No, thanks." She smiled at her friend. "I'll get a hotel." She had money but she hated to waste it on that.

"What about staying at your mom and dad's house."

"It's an hour away from where I work."

"Take some time off."

"I can't. I was just given a new project. It's going to take months to sort through all that data."

"You should stay with Adrian."

"No." She glanced his way. He stood at the bar, chatting with the bartender, a huge smile on his face.

"As a friend. He's a nice guy, Ellie."

"I can't go through this again and even if I could I don't think I'm still welcome."

"Why?"

"Look at him." There was no doubt that he'd be bringing the bartender home with him tonight and she wasn't going to be in the other room while they fucked on the couch or against the wall.

"Yeah, so?"

"He has plans tonight."

"Doing what?"

"Her." She made an obvious glance at the bartender.

"No." Alison stared at them. "You think?"

"Yes." She had no idea how Alison could be so obtuse.

"Ask him."

"If he's going home with the bartender? No, thanks. I'll pass."

"No." Alison gave her a disgusted look. "Ask him if he really meant that you could stay in the guest room for a few days."

"I could always stay in my apartment tonight and most of tomorrow."

"You know Marc's coming back tonight and you don't need to be there with him and his new woman."

"I know.'" She was pretty sure she'd puke if she had to listen to them go at it.

"Ask him," prodded Alison.

"I don't want to." It was embarrassing and humiliating.

"You're so stubborn. You'd rather spend a fortune staying at a hotel than—"

"I don't want to spend that kind of money but there's no point in asking him. He's going to say no, and I don't blame him." She stood. "I haven't been very nice to him."

"Apologize by sleeping with him." Alison grinned. "He'll forgive you. Men will forgive pretty much anything for sex."

"I can't, Alison. I can't do that again."

"That bad, huh? I thought you were kidding about him being bad in the sack."

"I was. Sex with him is great but I can't be with a guy like him. You saw the mess my life is now because of Marc. I'm tired of being with someone for years only to discover that he's cheating on me. I can't do it again. I won't do it again." No matter how much she wanted to.

"Are you sure Adrian's like that?"

"Look at him." She let her eyes linger on his body. Just the sight of him made her ache. If she thought about their times together, she was practically a cat in heat. "I can't stay with him. I just can't." If she did, she was pretty sure she'd jump him the first chance she got.

CHAPTER 43: ADRIAN

Adrian glanced at Ellie as she walked toward the restroom. The more he drank the angrier he got with her. He couldn't believe she thought he was just like Marc. He'd done nothing but be nice to her.

"I need to talk to you. Now." Alison grabbed his arm and he let her pull him to an empty table in the back.

"What's up?" He sat, knowing this was about Ellie and he wasn't really in the mood to hear it.

"You need to convince Ellie to stay with you for a few days."

"I offered. Nothing else I can do." It was all he was going to say about that.

"She thinks you're mad at her and—"

"She's a smart one." He took a sip of his beer.

"Give her a break." Alison frowned at him.

"A break? *Me* give her a break? She thinks I'm like Marc."

"Yeah"—Alison made a face—"it sucks but prove her wrong."

"I don't see why I should have to prove anything. She

should judge me by my actions not my looks." Damn, now he sounded like one of his sisters.

"Your actions. Let's see. You picked her up at a sex club while playing a sex game."

"She wanted to play." Actually, he wasn't certain about that.

"No, she wanted to get back at Marc," said Alison. "And the next time you saw her, you wagered with her for sex."

"I dropped that bet and I also drove out of my way to take her home for Christmas."

"Where you weaseled your way in to meet her family when you knew she didn't want you to do that, especially after giving her that hickey."

"I didn't weasel...She mentioned the hickey, huh?" He was still proud of that.

"Yeah, she did." It was clear by Alison's tone that it hadn't been a good thing. "Then, let's see?" She pretended to be deep in thought. "The next time the two of you met didn't you beat the shit out of her ex?"

"I did enjoy that." He smiled into his beer.

"I would've loved to have seen it." She slapped his arm. "Next time, call me."

"Will do." He was looking forward to a next time.

"Thank you, but can you see where I'm going with this?"

He frowned. "No. Everything I did was reasonable for the situation."

"Everything you did proves you're an alpha-male

caveman."

"I walk her to her door to make sure she's safe even when I'm pissed at her."

"Caveman." Alison grunted like a monkey.

"I helped her move today."

"Flexing those muscles. Caveman."

"Fine. I'm a caveman. So what? It doesn't make me a jerk."

"I know that, and you know that, but all Ellie's ever been around are cavemen who are jerks. Show her you're a different kind of caveman. Let her stay with you. It'll only be a few days, maybe a week at the most."

"I offered." He wasn't sure he wanted her at his place. They'd fuck and then she'd claim he was a caveman because he liked to fuck hard and often.

"Offer again." Alison's eyes widened. "She's coming. Please think about it." She darted away, staying along the back wall until she made it to her table.

His eyes moved to Ellie like a compass to due north. She glanced at the bar and then back again, her gaze slower now, going over every person. Was she looking for him? He stood and walked toward his friends. Her eyes met his for one second before she looked away and headed to her table.

Now, he was positive. She'd been searching for him. Maybe Alison was right and there was a chance that she could lose her prejudices and see him for who he was. His head told him to let her go. She wasn't worth the risk because he was positive that the more he got to know her, the more he'd want her, and he wasn't sure she'd feel the same way about him.

CHAPTER 44: ELLIE

Ellie waved over the waitress. "Can I get my tab, please?"

"Sure, honey." The waitress walked away.

"Are you going to talk to him?" asked Alison.

"Of course." Ellie pulled out her credit card.

"Good. You're being smart for once."

"Hey." Ellie gave her friend a dirty look. "I'm always smart and I'm going to thank him for his help today and say goodbye."

"Arghh. You're so stubborn." Alison dropped her head on the table. "Listen to me for once," she mumbled, head still down.

"Leaving already?"

Ellie jumped at the sound of Adrian's voice, her body getting tingly. Part of her had been waiting all night for him to come and talk to her. The other part had been glad he hadn't. "Yeah. Thank you for your help. You and your friends. I never could've gotten it done without you."

"You're welcome." He glanced at Alison who was now sitting up like a normal person. "Can we have a minute?" Adrian pulled out a chair and sat.

"Sure. Yep. Absolutely." Alison stood and hurried over to the bar.

The waitress put the bill down in front of Ellie. "I'll be back to pick it up."

"No, wait. Give me one minute." Ellie flipped the bill over, glancing at the total. This couldn't be everything. "Uhm, I don't think it's right. You're missing some drinks." The pizzas, French fries and wings were all on the bill but only three pitchers of beer.

"It's right. Just pay it," said Adrian.

"It can't be. I know you guys drank more beer than this."

"For this bill and mine." He handed his card to the waitress.

"No. I'll pay..." But the waitress walked away. "You aren't paying for all of this. You helped me."

"Let it go." He sounded as frustrated as she felt.

"I pay my way."

"Fine. You can pay me back."

"Adrian, I'm not...we're not..." She wasn't having sex with him for a bar tab.

"What a dirty mind you have." He chuckled. "I meant with money."

"Oh. Of course. I didn't mean..."

"Plus, that little tab would barely cover the cost of a kiss from you."

"What's that supposed to mean?" She wasn't sure if she should be insulted or if it was an odd compliment.

"Forget it. Forget I said it."

"No. What did you mean by that?"

"It's not important because there won't be any more of these games between us."

Now, she was really suspicious.

"I think you should stay with me until you find a place but no sex." He was serious. "I don't care how much you beg."

She laughed but he didn't even smirk. "I won't beg."

"Good because that'd be embarrassing."

"Don't worry."

The waitress came back and handed Adrian his card and a slip. He signed it leaving a huge tip. Ellie didn't usually look at that stuff on someone else's bill but since she was paying him back, it was okay.

"Thanks, Adrian," said the waitress before walking away.

"I'm paying my share of that tip too."

"Fine." He sighed. "You can pay me when we get to my apartment."

"Thank you but I don't—"

"Ellie, it's stupid to waste your money on a hotel. I have an empty room. You can even have your own bathroom. I always use the one in the master bedroom. Just stay at my place."

"You won't mind that we aren't…you know."

"I'll survive." He started to take her hand and then stopped. "We're friends. Nothing more. No benefits. No touching. Nothing but roommates."

"You really mean it?"

"Absolutely."

"How much will you want for rent?"

"Nothing."

"I'm paying rent."

He sighed again. "We can work that out later. Let's go home."

That word, home, coming from this man made her heart swell like the Grinch's and her blood run cold. It was an illusion, a fairy tale except hers never ended with happily ever after.

****

Thanks for reading **A Banging New Year** *(Hot Holidays series book 2)*. Keep reading for an excerpt from Cupid's Misfire.

Grab Cupid's Misfire for Adrian and Ellie's Happily Ever After

https://ellisoday.com/books/cupids-misfire

Excerpt from Cupid's Misfire (Hot Holidays book 3)

Adrian pulled into the parking lot at his apartment and took a moment to prepare himself before entering hell. The first week or so of living with Ellie had been torture but nothing he couldn't handle. Now, he walked around in a constant state of arousal and it was all her fault.

Instead of wearing big, baggy sweats and an even baggier T-shirt with her breasts strapped down so tight by some kind of running bra or torture device that they didn't even move, she pranced around the house in yoga pants and a spaghetti string tank top. He'd go to bed every night with his dick talking to his bellybutton and a headache from his eyes bouncing back and forth between her tits and her pussy. If he looked hard enough, he was pretty sure he could make out those pussy lips. Fuck, he wanted to kiss them again.

On top of all that torture, she seemed oblivious to him. She used to be nervous when he'd stand or sit too close and every now and then, he'd catch her staring liked she wanted to tear his clothes off and devour him. He'd prayed many times that she would. He wouldn't be breaking his rule if she made the first move. Actually, he'd be the bigger person by modifying his rule for her—in this case from no sex to sex all the fucking time.

He groaned and made his way to his apartment. He had an hour or so before she arrived. He could shower and jerk off just like every other fucking day. He opened the door and almost turned around. His nightmare had begun early.

Ellie sat on the couch in short shorts. He was pretty sure if she spread her legs, he'd be able to see the hair on her pussy. As a matter of fact, he'd see it up close because if she spread those legs, he'd be on her like a starving man.

"Hey." She smiled up at him.

Find out what happens next
https://ellisoday.com/books/cupids-misfire

Or do you want to read about how Ethan and La Petite Mort Club helped to save Liz and Craig's marriage?

Or maybe you want to meet more of the gorgeous and kinky men and women of La Petite Mort Club.

Just check out the excerpts. There's one for the following books:

A Merry Masquerade for Christmas. Craig and Liz are headed for a divorce over a misunderstanding. Can one night of kinky fun at a masquerade ball save their marriage?

His Sub (free ebook) — Terry's a dominant but Maggie's not his usual sub. She's a curvy, single mother of three who needs a dominant's guidance more than any woman he's ever met. However, she insists on fighting him every step of the way..

Interviewing for her Lover (free ebook) — Nick's the consummate playboy. Sarah is looking for a lover for a few nights. They should be perfect for each other and they are. Too perfect. Their chemistry is off-the-charts explosive. Will they be able to walk away after only six nights of fantasies? (this book is the first of their six nights together).

The Voyeur (free ebook)–See how Patrick (Adrian's boss) and Annie meet. She's a maid who likes to watch people having sex at the Club. He's given the job of keeping her out of trouble, but he's the biggest danger to her because no matter how hard he tries, he just can't keep his hands off her.

Plus, if you sign up for my newsletter, you can get the

entire Six Nights of Sin series for free (all six nights of Nick and Sarah's contract—every delicious fantasy) as a thank you gift.

Click here to join and get your free book.

Go to my website or email me for details:

www.EllisODay.com

authorEllisOday@gmail.com

Liz shoved the mop across the floor. She always cleaned when she was upset. Her house was going to be spotless. This was all so unfair and so typical. Craig was going to a party—a masked party on Christmas Eve. She'd be sitting home, crying and watching *It's a Wonderful Life,* while her husband would be having the time of his life with some other woman. She snorted. Nothing new there. He'd been doing it for years.

Her phone beeped. That'd better not be him needing something else. She'd skewer him with the mop handle if she had to see him again.

She put the mop down and walked into the kitchen to grab her phone. Damn, he'd looked good yesterday—his body strong and lean, his dark brown hair a little too long. When she'd turned and he'd been looking at her with desire...no hot lust, she'd almost fallen into his arms. She hated that she still wanted him. He'd never change. He'd always cheat—her father had, her sister's husband had. Craig wouldn't be any different, especially with a membership to that club.

She grabbed her phone off the counter and stared at her messages. This had to be a mistake, but it wasn't. It was a blessing.

Come and check out The Christmas Eve Bash. Mask Required. Clothing Optional. Doors open at 6 pm. Non-members show this message for entry.

This had to be the party Craig was attending. Ethan must've forgotten to remove her from the potential client list. It was her own Christmas miracle. She hurried to the garage. She had to find a mask. She was going to show Craig that she wasn't just his wife—soon to be ex-wife. She was a woman who needed a man and she was still attractive enough to get one.

Find out what happens next.

https://ellisoday.com/books/a-merry-masquerade-for-

Ellis O. Day

christmas/

Free - His Sub

Terry wandered through the crowd of well-dressed women and men at La Petite Mort Club. It was the same scene every time Ethan, his friend and owner of the Club, threw one of these events. The members mingled with the newbies, hoping to snag something different or someone interesting.

Ethan strolled casually toward him, a ready smile on his face as he greeted his guests. "Terry, about time you made it down here."

"Like you can talk." His friend spent most of his time

in the back office, watching the Club on monitors.

"I've been mingling for over an hour."

"It's your business not mine." He leaned against the balustrade, peering down on the crowd.

"True, but you could sell your practice and buy me out."

"And run this place?" He laughed. "No thank you." He tossed back his scotch. "I spend enough time here as it is." He used to practically live here except when he was at the office or in court, but lately he'd been staying home more.

"Good turn out tonight." Ethan waved at a waitress and a moment later they each had another drink.

"Yeah, but I don't see one interesting person in this crop of wannabe members."

"And you can tell if someone is interesting just by looking at them?"

"I can tell not one of them has an original thought. Look at them. They're all in red." The Club was awash in a sea of red dresses—short, long, dark, light but always red.

"It is a Valentine's Day party."

"I know but you'd think one woman"—he held up his finger—"one would consider that everyone else would be in red and wear a different color."

"There are some pinks out there."

"Same thing, just lighter."

Ethan grabbed his phone from his pocket and looked at the text, frowning.

"Problem?" The Club was usually a safe place but on open night events, when Ethan allowed non-members access in order to recruit new members, the place could get dangerous.

"A little skirmish over a woman." Ethan grinned, his blue eyes sparkling as a couple of young guys hurried past them, almost tripping in their haste to stay close to a group of very attractive women. "These youngsters haven't learned that sharing is more fun."

He ignored Ethan's teasing. He'd taken a lot of shit from Ethan, Nick and even Patrick because he wasn't into the sharing thing. He preferred it to be him and one woman, one sweet, little sub. Since he was in no mood to listen to any more crap, he'd change the subject. "Those kids barely look old enough to drink."

"You're showing your age." Ethan patted his shoulder. "You should find some nice, young thing and teach her how to please her master."

"Maybe I will, if any of them show enough originality to dress in something other than red."

"I've got to go and sort out this problem." Ethan slid his phone into his pocket. "I'll find you later. If you find that elusive non-red dress, I'd suggest we share but..." He chuckled as he headed down the stairs, maneuvering through the crowd like he had nowhere to go, when in reality he was heading for the back—the playrooms.

Terry's eyes stopped and lingered on the new hire, Desiree, who was moving around the room, talking and flirting with all the men and some women. She was interesting—exotic and smart—but there was a shrewdness behind her eyes that he'd learned a long time ago to avoid.

A woman like her had an agenda and she stuck with it, no matter what.

Someone slammed into his back, causing his drink to spill down his front, staining his shirt and suit.

"Oh...oh, I'm so sorry."

He spun around and encountered a red dress and breasts—milky white and lush. The skin would be fragrant and softer than rose petals.

"Oh. Your shirt. Let me get something to wipe that up."

He forced his eyes away from those lovely breasts. Her hair was a rich mahogany. It'd probably hang past her shoulders in waves of curly silk but right now it was piled haphazardly on her head in what had been some kind of elegant style before disobedient strands had escaped their restraint. She looked mussed and damnit, he wanted to be the one to muss her.

"Paper towels? Napkins?" She glanced around and then hurried over to the bar.

She was short and curvy—her body succulent, ripe and he'd bet juicy. She grabbed a stack of napkins and headed for him. Her dress was too tight, like she'd recently gained some weight. He usually went for the tall, athletic types but for some reason his dick had picked this woman.

She returned to his side and dabbed at the wetness on his shirt and jacket as if she actually gave a shit about his clothes. This was no subtle caress, no flirtation—just indifferent efficiency.

"I'm so sorry." She wadded the napkins in her hand,

still patting at his clothes.

"You said that already." His words came out gruffer than he'd meant. No one treated him with disinterest. He was a rich, successful, attractive man and she was treating him like a child. He wanted to pull up her—unfortunately, red—dress and fuck her right here. They were at the Club. It wasn't out of the question.

Her hand froze. "Oh." Her large hazel eyes looked startled and then hurt. "Sorry. Ah, excuse me." She headed toward the stairs, dropping the wet napkins in the trash before disappearing in the crowd.

He turned around, so he could see the first floor and waited for her to appear. She hurried across the downstairs room, bumping and stumbling through the crowd. A lone, scared, little rabbit in a room full of predators. She stopped for a moment, scanning the crowd as if searching for someone.

"Who are you looking for, little rabbit?" he mumbled to himself. "A husband? Boyfriend?" He grinned as he lifted his scotch to his lips. "Girlfriend?" He frowned at the empty glass. "You spilled my drink. I'll forgive you, but it's going to cost you." He waved at one of the waitresses. "Everything has a price, little rabbit." As one of the best divorce lawyers in town, he knew that better than anyone.

The waitress brought him another drink. He paid, giving her a large tip before turning to find his little rabbit. He took a sip of the scotch, enjoying the smooth burn and his lush little bunny's journey through La Petite Mort Club. She froze in her tracks, her jaw dropping open as she gazed at a threesome on one of the couches.

The woman was sandwiched between two men, stroking one's cock as the other man fondled her beneath her red dress. The man behind her looked up and said something to the little rabbit. Her face heated and Terry's eyes dropped to her chest. Yep, they were a pretty shade of pink but what he really wanted to know was if the color matched her pussy.

She stumbled away from the threesome, bumping into another man. It was Richard, who stopped her from falling and then immediately let her go, stepping away. She was safe with Richard. As a member of the Club and a gentleman, he knew that safewords were law and consent was absolutely necessary. She said something to Richard and continued through the Club, disappearing in the crowd.

"You're not getting away that easily." He followed along on the upper floor, keeping her in sight. He had no idea why but he wanted her. Maybe it was simply because she was different than everyone else here.

He took another sip of his drink. It was obviously the little rabbit's first time at a place like this but she didn't seem eager to participate or interested in watching. She truly seemed to be looking for someone specific—not just someone to fuck. Well, she'd found the latter because he was going to fuck her. In the office he followed his head but at La Petite Mort Club his cock was king.

She headed toward the playrooms. There was no way he was going to miss this. He sauntered down the stairs, grabbing another drink on the way. She wasn't hard to follow. She left a path of irritated people in her wake as she bumped into them and apologized profusely before hurrying forward. Her full, round hips swayed under her tight, red dress that'd seen better days—hem frayed and at least five years out of style. Not that he minded, especially the snug fit of the cloth, but his women were usually much more put tougher.

They were the CEO types—women who thrived on being in charge. He enjoyed teaching them how much fun turning over control could be. When they were with him, he was their dom, their master and he made sure they loved every second. He told them when to kneel, when to suck, when to spread their legs or ass and when to come. The more power they had in their everyday life the more they craved bowing to his wishes. His little rabbit wouldn't know what power was. She was a hot mess of a woman. Still, his dick wanted her, so his dick would have her.

She was hurrying out of the first playroom when he entered the hallway. Her eyes were huge and her cheeks were on fire. She ducked into the next room and quickly came out—even redder than before.

"Excuse me." He'd offer his assistance in her search. She'd be grateful. He could capitalize on that unless she was looking for her husband or boyfriend. He wasn't in the mood to share. He would, however, allow the other man to watch. He could give the guy some pointers on how to take care of his wife because this woman obviously needed guidance.

"You?" Her eyes narrowed.

That wasn't the reaction he was used to. Women usually purred for him.

"Are you following me?"

"What would you do if I said I was?" He took a step toward her.

"I'd scream. There are bouncers here. I saw them."

Lord, she was cute. "Yes, but if they came running at every little scream they'd die of exhaustion."

As if to emphasis his point a woman screamed in ecstasy. His little rabbit's face heated and she averted her gaze.

"Who are you looking for?" He ran his finger lightly down her cheek. Her skin was as smooth as porcelain but much warmer and softer.

"Ah…" Her breath hitched, making her breasts swell dangerously above her gown.

He could have her out of it in a minute. The skin would be even softer than that on her face. "Did you lose your husband?"

"No." She licked her lips.

There was no way he could let that offer pass. He slowly bent, giving her time to refuse him. He may command his women but he made sure they always wanted it first. Her eyes dropped to his mouth and he couldn't help a slight smirk. She wanted this as much as he did. He moved closer and let his lips rest gently on hers. He'd take it slow, make her yearn for him and then he'd make her obey.

"What are you doing?" She turned her head.

"Kissing you." His lips brushed against her cheek. He wasn't about to lose ground.

"Why?" She turned again, her eyes meeting his.

The confusion in her hazel gaze was as obvious as the hideous dress on her gorgeous body. She may remind him of a rabbit but she couldn't be that naive. She had to be in her mid to late thirties.

He should use flowery words—tell her she was beautiful, desirable—but that wasn't him. Blunt was the kindest word to describe him. "Because, I want to."

"You don't even know me."

He was losing ground. The interest in her face was being replaced with disgust. "No, but I know I want you." Damn, he shouldn't have said that.

"Well, too bad." She pushed on his chest and he stepped back, letting her pass.

"This is a sex club, you know." He followed. "If you aren't here for sex, why are you here?"

She spun around. "I'm quite aware of what this place is and just because I don't want you, a stranger to...to"—she waved her hand about—"in the hallway."

He laughed. "We wouldn't be the first. There are people fucking in the main room."

"I know. I saw." Her cheeks heated.

He stepped closer. "You are adorable." He touched a strand of hair that was resting on her shoulder. It was like satin.

"I'm a mess." She pulled her hair free from his fingers.

"A hot mess. A fiery, hot, sexy mess." He moved

closer with every other word. "One I want to fuck, right now."

Her eyes hardened. "Too bad because I don't"—again she waved her hand about—"you know, with strangers in the hallway." She shoved his chest again.

He took a small step back but he wasn't giving up yet. "We can go to a private room."

"No."

Shit. By the look on her face, he'd just made a bigger blunder.

"Let me go." She pushed him again.

Damn. She'd said the worst three words in the English language besides I love you. He moved away, releasing her for the moment. "Sorry."

She harrumphed.

"I made a mistake."

"Yes, you did." She hurried down the hallway but not before he'd seen the look of hurt in her large eyes.

"What the fuck do you want from me? I made a mistake and apologized." He trailed after her.

"I want you to leave me alone. Please. Go away."

He stopped. His little rabbit was running but perhaps, he shouldn't chase. She darted down a hallway toward the hardcore BDSM rooms.

Normally, she'd be fine—embarrassed but fine. Except with all the newbies here, tonight wasn't a normal night. He hurried after her. "Hey, I don't think you want to go—"

"Leave me alone." She walked faster. "I need to find my friend and get out of here."

"Okay, but I don't—"

"Go away." She sounded both mad and as if she were going to cry.

"Suit yourself, but I warned you."

She strode into the closest room. He should leave. Let her find out that he wasn't the worst thing in a place like this, not in a long shot, but his feet followed her. She was his little rabbit. He'd found her. No one else was going to enjoy her until he'd had his taste.

"Vicky? Vicky? Are you in here?"

He stepped into the room, staying in the shadows. She was looking around in the dark for her friend. It only took a moment for one of the six guys to notice the little rabbit who'd stumbled into their den.

"Shit," he mumbled. Not one of those guys was a regular.

Grab your free copy and find out what happens next.
You can find the book on my website
https://ellisoday.com/books/free-his-sub/

Free: Interviewing For Her Lover

"Do I have to take off my clothes?" Sarah tugged on the hem of her black dress. It was shorter and lower cut in the front than she normally wore, but the Viewing was about finding a man for sex and according to Ethan men liked to look.

"No." Ethan turned her away from the door and forced her to look at him. "You don't have to do anything you don't want to do."

She stared into his blue eyes. Why couldn't he be interested in her? She'd only met with him five or six times, but she trusted him. He ran his business, La Petite

Mort Club, very professionally and he was gorgeous with his sandy brown hair, strong cheekbones and vibrant blue eyes. Sex between them would be good. Easy. He was attractive and...not for her. She didn't want decent sex or good sex, she wanted mind blowing, screaming orgasms and that wouldn't happen between him and her because there was no chemistry, no attraction.

"Listen to me." He moved his hands to her shoulders and gave her a gentle shake. "You aren't selling yourself to the highest bidder. You're looking for a partner. One who'll"—he grinned—"turn you on in ways you can't even imagine."

She glanced at the door where the men waited. Waited for her. Waited to decide if they wanted to fuck her. "I'm a bit nervous."

"About what?"

This was embarrassing, but she'd been honest with him up to this point. She'd had to be. He was helping her...had helped her to choose the five men in the other room. "What if none of them..."

"They will want you." He touched her chin, turning her face toward him. "A few of them may back out after this but not because they don't want you."

"Yeah, right."

"I'm only going to say this once. You're beautiful and different, unique."

"That's not necessarily a good thing." She had long legs and a nice body—trim and firm—but with her auburn hair and green eyes she was cute at best, not gorgeous. The men she'd chosen were all rich, good looking and powerful. They could have anyone they wanted.

"It's exactly what they want, or most of them anyway." He took her hand and led her closer to the door.

She leaned on his arm, hating these shoes. She should've stuck with her flats but Ethan had given her a list of what she should wear and high heels were on the top. She'd found the smallest heels in the store and by Ethan's look when he'd first seen her she might've been better off going barefoot. He'd met her at the private entrance and his gaze had been appreciating as it'd skimmed over her dress until he got to her feet. Then he'd frowned and shook his head.

"Finding the right men for you wasn't easy." He stopped at the door.

"Thanks a lot." She shifted away from him, his words hurting a little. She hadn't been sure of her appeal to the opposite sex in a long time, not since the early years with Adam.

"It's not because you aren't beautiful but because you want to be dominated and you want to dominate—"

"I do not want to dominate." All she could picture was a woman in black leather with a whip and that wasn't her, not at all.

"If you say so." He smiled a little. "But, you do want to lead the scene. Right? Because that's what—"

"Yes." Her face was red. She could feel it. She didn't want to talk about her fantasies again. It'd been embarrassing enough the first time, but he'd had to know what she wanted to compile a list of candidates.

"Most at the club are either doms or subs. Very few are switches." His eyes raked over her. "That's what's so special about you. You want it all and…that's what made choosing these men difficult."

He'd given her a selection of twenty-two men who might be interested in what she wanted. She'd narrowed it down to seven. Two had been uninterested when he'd approached. That'd left her with the five who'd see her in person for the first time tonight, but she wouldn't see them. That'd come after the Viewing when she interviewed any who were still interested.

"Remember what you want. This is your deal. You call the shots. At least a little." He kissed her forehead. "But don't refuse to give them anything. You don't want a submissive."

"No." That didn't turn her on at all and she only had eight weeks. One night each week for two months before she'd go back to her lonely life, her lonely bed, dreaming of Adam.

"You can do this." He pulled a flask from his jacket and unscrewed the lid. "For courage."

"Thanks." She took a large swallow, the brandy too thick and sweet for her taste but it was better than nothing.

"Now, go find your lover."

She laughed a little but sadness swept through her. There'd be no love between this man and herself. This would be sex, fucking. That's all. The only man she'd ever love, her only lover, was dead. This was purely physical. "Thank you again." She stood on tip-toe and kissed his cheek. He may be gorgeous and run a sex club but he was a good man, a good friend.

She turned and opened the door and walked into the room, trying to stay balanced on these stupid heels. Men wouldn't find them so attractive if they had to wear them. The room was dark except for one light highlighting a small platform. That was for her. She stepped up onto the small stage. The room was silent but they were there, above her, hidden behind the one-way mirrors, watching and deciding if they wanted to take the next step—to eventually take her.

She stared into the blackness of the room. It wasn't huge but its emptiness made it seem vast. She glanced upward, the light making her squint and she quickly stared back into the darkness. This was arranged for them to see her. That was it. She'd get no glimpse of them yet. She'd seen their pictures, chosen them but meeting them in person would be different. A picture couldn't tell her their smell or the sound of their voices.

She tugged at her dress where it hugged her hips, wishing the questions would start, but there was only silence. She shifted, the heels already killing her feet. Ethan hadn't liked them and if they weren't going to impress, she might as well take them off. She moved to the back of the stage, leaned against the wall and removed her shoes. As she returned to the center of the stage a man spoke, his voice loud and commanding almost echoing throughout the room.

"Don't stop there. Take off your dress."

She bent, placing her shoes on the floor. That wasn't part of the deal. She wasn't going to undress in front of five men, only one. Only the one she chose. She straightened. "No."

"What?" He was surprised and not happy.

"I said no. That's not part of the Viewing."

"I want to see what I'm getting."

She stared up toward the windows, squinting a little. She couldn't tell from where the voice had come. The speaker system made it sound as if it were coming from God himself. "And you will if I pick you."

Another man laughed.

"It's not funny. She's disobedient," said the man with the loud voice.

"Not always. I can be obedient." These men liked to be in control but sometimes, so did she.

"Will you raise your dress? Just a little," asked another voice.

"Didn't you see enough in the photos?" She'd applied a few months ago for this one-time contract. She'd been excited and nervous when she'd received the acceptance email with an appointment for a photography session. She'd never had her picture professionally taken, since she didn't count school portraits or the ones her parents had had done at JCPenny's. She'd been anxious and a little turned on imaging wearing her new lingerie in front of a strange man, so she'd been disappointed to find the photographer was an elderly woman, but the lady had put her at ease and the photos had turned out better than she'd expected. She glanced up at the mirrors, hoping she wasn't disappointing all the men. That'd be too embarrassing.

"Those were...nice, but I'd like to see the real thing before deciding if you're worth my time."

She raised a brow. "You can always leave." She shouldn't antagonize him. She was sure the bossy man had already decided against committing to this agreement. Disobedience didn't appeal to him. That left four. If she didn't pick any of them, she could go through the process again, but she didn't think she would.

The man chuckled slightly. "I know that, but I haven't decided I don't want to fuck you. Not yet, anyway."

The word, so harsh and vulgar excited her. It was the truth. That was what she, what they were all deciding. Who'd get to fuck her. It was what she wanted, what she'd agreed to do, and as much as she dreaded it, she wanted it. She was tired of being alone. She missed having a man inside her—his tongue and fingers and cock.

"Do any of you have any questions?" She clasped her dress at her waist and slowly gathered it upward, displaying more and more of her long legs. She ran. They were in shape. The men would like them.

"Lower your top," said the same man who'd told her to take off her dress.

She didn't like him. If he didn't back out, she'd have Ethan remove him from her list. He was too commanding. He'd never allow her to be in control.

"I don't know if he's done looking at my legs yet."

She continued raising the dress until her black and green lace panties were almost exposed.

"Very nice and thank you," said the polite man.

"You're welcome." This man might work. She shifted the dress up another inch before dropping it, giving them a glance at her panties.

"Now, your top," said the bossy guy.

She lowered her spaghetti string off one shoulder, letting the dress dip, but not enough to show anything besides the side of her bra.

"More," he said.

"No." She raised the strap, covering herself. She didn't like this man and wished he'd leave. She'd kick him out but that wasn't part of the process and they were very firm about their rules at this club.

"He got to see your pussy. Why don't I get to see your tits?"

"You got to see as much as he did." She was ready to move on. She bent and picked up her shoes. "If there's nothing else, gentleman, we can set up times for the interview process."

"Turn around," said another man.

It was a command, but she didn't mind. There was a politeness to his order and something about the texture of his voice caused an ache between her thighs. There was a caress in his tone but with an edge and a promise of a good hard fuck.

"Are you going to obey?" His words were whisper soft and smooth.

"Yes." That was going to be part of this too. Her commanding and him commanding. She dropped her shoes and turned.

"Raise you dress again."

She looked over her shoulder at where she imagined he sat watching her.

"Please." There was humor in his tone.

She smiled and slowly gathered the dress upward. She stopped right below the curve of her bottom.

"More. Please." There was a little less humor in his voice.

She wanted to show him her ass. She wanted to show that voice everything but not with the others around. This would be just her and one man, one stranger. That was one of her rules. "No. Only if you're picked do you get to see any more of me than you have." She dropped her dress, grabbed her shoes and walked off the stage and out the door.

She was going to have sex with a stranger. She was going to live out her fantasies for eight nights with a man she didn't know and would never really know, but she wasn't going to lose who she was. She'd keep her honor and her dignity which meant she had to pick a man who'd agree with her rules.

Get your free copy and find out what happens next.

https://books2read.com/u/3nYKo6

Free: The Voyeur

Annie finished making the bed and gathered the sheets from the floor, keeping them as far away from her body as possible. These sex rooms were disgusting and Ethan was a jerk making her work as a maid. She almost had her Bachelor's Degree in Culinary Arts, but he'd refused to hire her for the kitchen—too many men in the kitchen. The only job he'd give her at La Petite Mort Club was as a maid and unfortunately, she needed the money too badly to refuse.

She stuffed the dirty sheets into the cart and hurried out the door. She had almost thirty minutes before she had to be at the next "sex room." She hid the cart in a closet and darted down a back hallway, staying clear of the cameras. Julie, the woman who supervised the daytime maids, was a real bitch. If she were caught sneaking away from her duties, she'd be assigned to the orgy rooms every day. Right now, they all took turns cleaning that nightmare. She swore they should get hazard pay to even go in those rooms.

She slipped through a doorway and hurried to the one-way mirror. She stared at the couple in the next room. From her first day here, she'd been curious about the activities at the club. She was twenty-four and wasn't a virgin but she'd never, ever done some of these things.

The woman in the room below was tied to a table, legs spread and wearing some sort of leather outfit that left her large breasts free and her crotch exposed. She had shaved her pussy and her pink lower lips were swollen and glistening from her excitement. The man strolled around the table as if he had all night. He still had his pants on but had removed his shirt. His arms and chest were well defined but he had a slight paunch. His erection tented his pants and Annie felt wetness pool between her legs. She had no idea why watching this turned her on but it did. Ever since she'd accidentally barged in on that guy and girl in the Interview room, she couldn't stop watching.

The man below ran his hand up the woman's inner thigh, glancing over her pussy. The woman thrust her hips upward and Annie ran her own hand between her legs. The man's mouth moved but Annie couldn't hear anything and then he slapped the woman across the thigh hard enough to leave a red mark. Annie jumped. She wasn't into that, but she couldn't stop watching the woman's face. At first, it'd contorted in pain but then it'd morphed into pleasure. The man hit her again and then bent, kissing the red welts—running his tongue across them as his fingers squeezed her nipple.

Annie clutched her thighs together, searching for some relief. Her panties were soaked. It wouldn't take but a few strokes to make her come. She started to slide her hand into her pants.

"Having fun?" asked a deep voice from behind her.

She spun around, her heart dropping into her stomach. "Ah...I was just finishing cleaning in here." Damn, she should've closed the door but she hadn't expected anyone in this area. The rooms were off limits on this floor until tonight and she was the only one assigned to clean here.

He shut the door and locked it before strolling toward her. She'd seen him around the Club, but more than that she remembered him from the military photos her brother, Vic, had sent to her. She carried one of the three of them—Vic, Ethan and this guy, Patrick—in her purse. He'd been attractive in the picture, but now that he was older and in person he was gorgeous. He had dark green eyes, brown hair and a perfect body. He stopped so close to her his chest almost brushed against her breasts. She was pretty sure it would if she inhaled deeply. She really wanted to take that deep breath and feel his hard chest against her breasts.

"Don't let me stop you from enjoying the show."

"I...I wasn't. I should go." She started to walk past him but he grabbed her hand.

His grip was warm and strong but loose enough that she could pull free if she wanted. She didn't. Even though she only knew him from her brother's pictures and letters, she'd had many fantasies about him when she'd been in high school. Her gaze dropped to the front of his pants and her mouth almost watered. He was definitely interested. She dragged her eyes up his body, stopping on his face. He smiled at her.

"There's nothing to be embarrassed about. Watching turns us all on." He kissed the back of her hand and she jumped as his tongue darted out, tasting her skin.

"I...I should go." She didn't move.

"No, you should watch." He dropped her hand and grabbed her shoulders, gently turning her toward the mirror. He trailed his hands up and down her arms. "Watch."

The man in the other room was now sucking on the woman's breast as his fingers caressed her pussy.

"Would you like to hear them? Or do you like it quiet?" His voice was a rough whisper against her ear.

"Sound, please." She wanted to hear their gasps and moans. She wanted to close her eyes and pretend it was her. She shifted, squeezing her thighs together.

He chuckled as he moved away. She felt his absence to her bones. He'd been strong and warm behind her and for a moment she'd felt safe, safer than she had since her brother had come back from the war, broken and sad, and her father had started drinking again.

The woman's moans filled the room and Patrick came back to stand behind her, this time placing his hands on her waist.

"I'm Patrick," he said against her ear.

She couldn't take her eyes from the scene in front of her. The woman was almost coming as the man thrust his fingers inside of her.

"What's your name?" He nipped her neck and she jumped.

"I...I..." If she told him her name, he might say something to Ethan. Ethan would kill her if he knew she was in here watching.

"Tell me your name." His lips trailed along her neck and she tipped her head giving him better access.

The guy was kissing his way down the woman's body. Annie wanted to touch herself, to make herself come but Patrick was here.

He nibbled her ear. "Why won't you tell me your name?"

"I...I'll get in trouble." She rubbed her ass against his erection, hopefully giving him a hint.

"Tease." His hand drifted down her stomach, stopping right above where she wanted him to touch. "Tell me your name or I'll make you suffer." He unbuttoned her

pants and left his hand—warm, rough but immobile—
resting on her abdomen.

"I can't." She stood on tip-toe, hoping his hand
would lower a little but he was too tall or she was too short.
He had to be almost six foot and she was barely five-foot
four. "I could get fired and I need this job."

"Darling, Ethan won't fire you for fucking a
customer."

"We can't." She spun around. She hadn't thought
this through. He was her fantasy come to life and she
wanted him to be hers just for a moment, but Ethan would
find out and then she'd be in deep shit.

"Don't worry. I'm a member and you work here, so
we're both clean." He hesitated, his hands tightening on her
hips. "Are you protected?"

"What?" She had no idea what he was talking
about.

"Ethan makes sure everyone at the Club is clean but
only the...some of his employees are required to be on
birth control." He ran his hands up her sides, getting closer
and closer to her breasts. "Are you on birth control?" His
eyes darkened as they dropped to her tits. "If not, it's okay.
There are other things we can do."

Oh, she wanted to do everything his eyes promised,
but she couldn't. "No, I'll get in trouble. I need this job. I
have to go." She tried to move but her feet refused to obey,
so she just stared at his handsome face.

"Are you sure?" He bent so he was almost eye level
with her. "I promise. Ethan won't care. A lot of maids

become…change jobs. The pay's a lot better." His eyes roamed over her frame. "Especially, for someone as cute as you."

Ethan would kill her before letting her become one of his pleasure associates.

"I could talk to Ethan for you." His hands moved up her body, stopping right below her breasts.

Her nipples hardened and she forgot everything but what he was making her feel. He ran his thumb over one of them and she leaned closer, wanting him to do it again.

He did. He continued rubbing her nipple as he spoke. "I could persuade him to let me…handle your initiation into club life."

Her heart raced in her chest. It could be just her and him doing all these things she'd seen. Her pussy throbbed but she couldn't do it. She wouldn't do it. She couldn't have sex for money. Her parents were both dead but they'd never understand and she couldn't disappoint them. "No. I can't do that…not for money." Her eyes darted to the door. She needed to get out of there before she did something she'd regret.

"That's even better." He smiled as he stepped closer. "We can keep this between us. No money. Only a man and a woman." He leaned down and whispered in her ear, "Giving each other pleasure. A lot of pleasure. In ways you haven't even imagined."

There were moans from the other room and she glanced over her shoulder. The man's face was buried between the woman's thighs.

Patrick turned her around, pulling her against him and wrapping his arms around her waist. "Are you wet?"

"What? No." She struggled in his arms, her ass brushing against his erection again.

"Oh fuck. Do that again." He kissed her neck, open mouthed and hot.

She stopped trying to get away. She wanted this…this moment. She shouldn't but she did, so she wiggled her butt against him again. He was hard and long and her body ached for him. It'd been too long she'd had sex. She needed this.

"Would you like me to touch you?" His hands drifted over her hips and down her thighs.

She'd like him to do all sorts of things to her. She nodded.

"Say it." His words were a command she couldn't disobey.

"Yes."

"Yes, what?" He untucked her shirt from her pants.

"Touch me. Please." She was already pushing her hips toward his hand. She wanted his hand on her, his fingers inside of her.

"Are you wet?" he asked again.

She inhaled sharply as he unzipped her pants.

"Don't lie to me. I'll find out in a minute."

She'd never talked dirty during sex and she wasn't sure she was ready to do that with a stranger. Her heart skipped a beat. Maybe, she shouldn't be doing any of this with a stranger. She grabbed his hand. "Maybe, we shouldn't."

The woman below cried out and the man straightened, wiping his face and unbuttoning his pants.

"Watch. The main event is about to happen." Patrick's hot breath tickled her neck.

Her gaze locked on the man's penis. It was large and demanding. He straddled the woman, grabbing his cock.

"Don't you want to feel some of what they feel?" He nibbled on her ear and then neck. "I can help you."

She may not know him, but she trusted him. He was a former marine. He'd been a good friend of Vic's. He wouldn't hurt her and she needed to come. She loosened her grip, letting go of his hand. He slipped inside her pants, caressing her pussy through her underwear. His fingers were long and strong. She closed her eyes, leaning against him as he stroked her.

"You're already so wet and hot." His breath was a warm caress on her ear. "But, I'm going to make you wetter and then, I'm going to make you come." His other hand shoved her pants down, giving him more room to work. "Open your eyes and watch the show."

She did as he said. The man was inside the woman, thrusting hard and fast. The woman was moaning and trying to move but the restraints kept her mostly helpless.

"Fuck, you're soaked." Patrick's hand cupped her and she arched into his touch, rubbing her ass against his erection. He shoved his hand inside her underwear, his finger running along her folds until he slipped one inside.

"Oh." She grabbed his hand—not to push him away, but to make sure he didn't leave.

He smiled against her hair. "Don't worry, baby. I won't stop." He stroked his finger inside of her and his wrist brushed against her clit.

She needed more. She needed to touch him, feel him. She turned her head, wrapping her arms up and around his neck. He kissed her. It was desperate and wild, but he stopped too soon.

"They're almost done. You don't want to miss it."

She turned back to the mirror. The man below continued to fuck the woman as Patrick finger-fucked her. His other hand slipped under her shirt to her breast. His lips sucked her neck as he rocked his erection against her ass. He was everywhere, and she was so close. The muscles in her legs constricted. Her hips tipped upward.

"Wait, baby," he groaned in her ear, as he pushed a second finger inside of her. "Just a few more minutes."

His fingers were stretching her and it felt wonderful. She moaned, long and low as he thrust harder and faster, almost matching the pace of the man in the other room. She could almost imagine it was Patrick's cock and not his fingers inside of her.

"Oh…oh," she cried out. He was pushing her toward the edge. Her body was spiraling with each pump of his fingers. She was going to come—right here while watching that couple. It was so dirty and so wrong and it only made her hotter.

The woman below screamed and her body stiffened. The man thrust again and again and then grunted his release.

"Show's over." Patrick nipped her neck at the same time he pressed down on her clit with his thumb, sending her shooting into her orgasm.

She trembled and he pulled her close, his hand still cupping her pussy and his fingers still inside of her. When her heartbeat had settled, he removed his hand and bent, pulling off her shoes and removing her pants before lifting her and carrying her to the wall.

"My turn." He wrapped her legs around his waist.

Her phone rang. "My work phone. I…I have to answer it."

"When we're done." He unzipped his pants.

"Annie, answer the phone. I know you're around here. I can hear it ringing you stupid bitch," yelled Julie.

"Oh, shit." She shoved Patrick away, and ran across the room, grabbing her clothes off the floor. "It's my boss. She'll kill me if she finds me like this."

"I'll take care of Julie." He headed for the door, zipping up his fly. "Don't move." He grinned over his shoulder at her. "You can take off your pants again, but other than that, don't move."

"No. Please." She raced over to him, grabbing his arm. "I need this job." And Ethan could not find out about this.

"She won't fire you. She can't. Only Ethan can fire you." He bent and kissed her.

His lips were gentle and coaxing this time and her body swayed into him. He pulled her even closer and she could feel his cock, thick and heavy, pushing against her. Her pussy tightened again in anticipation.

"Damn it, Annie. This is going to be so much worse if I have to call your stupid phone again. Get out here!" Julie was only a few doors down.

She grabbed Patrick and tugged on his hand. "Please, hide." She glanced around, looking for somewhere that would conceal a six-foot muscular man.

"I'm not going to hide from Julie."

Get Your FREE Copy and find out what happens next.

HTTPS://BOOKS2READ.COM/U/BXQBMK

BOOKS BY ELLIS O. DAY
OR SEE THEM ALL ON MY WEBSITE
HTTPS://WWW.ELLISODAY.COM

LA PETITE MORT CLUB SERIES

THE BILLIONAIRE'S BABY
https://ellisoday.com/books/the-billionaires-baby
The Baby Bargain (book 1) (free)
https://books2read.com/thebabybargain
Making the Baby (book 2)
https://ellisoday.com/books/making-the-baby
The Baby Battle (book 3)
https://ellisoday.com/books/the-baby-battle
Having the Baby (book 4)
https://ellisoday.com/books/having-the-baby

HOT HOLIDAYS
Hot Holidays -The Complete Series: Books 1-3
https://ellisoday.com/books/hot-holidays-books-1-3
The Mistletoe Game (Book 1) (free)
http://mybook.to/mistletoegame
A Banging New Year (Book 2)
https://ellisoday.com/books/a-banging-new-year
Cupid's Misfire (Book 3)

https://ellisoday.com/books/cupids-misfire

SIX NIGHTS OF SIN SERIES
Six Nights of Sin -The Complete Series: Books 1-6
https://ellisoday.com/books/six-nights-of-sin-books-1-6/

Interviewing For Her Lover (Book 1) **(Free)**
https://books2read.com/u/3nYKo6
Taking Control (Book 2)
https://ellisoday.com/books/taking-control
School Fantasy (Book 3)
https://ellisoday.com/books/school-fantasy
Master-Slave Fantasy (Book 4)
https://ellisoday.com/books/master-slave-fantasy
Punishment Fantasy (Book 5)
https://ellisoday.com/books/punishment-fantasy
The Proposition (Book 6)
https://ellisoday.com/books/the-proposition

THE VOYEUR SERIES
THE VOYEUR **(FREE)**
https://books2read.com/u/bxqBMk
Watching The Voyeur (Book 2)
https://ellisoday.com/books/watching-the-voyeur
Touching The Voyeur (Book 3)
https://ellisoday.com/books/touching-the-voyeur
Loving The Voyeur (Book 4)

https://ellisoday.com/books/loving-the-voyeur

The Voyeur Series (Books 1-4)
https://ellisoday.com/books/the-voyeur-series-books-1-4/

SIX WEEKS OF SEDUCTION
https://ellisoday.com/books/six-weeks-of-seduction

A MERRY MASQUERADE FOR CHRISTMAS
https://ellisoday.com/books/a-merry-masquerade-for-christmas/

THE DOM'S SUBMISSION SERIES
The Dom's Submission Box Set (Books 1-3)
https://ellisoday.com/books/the-doms-submission-books-1-3/
His Sub (Book 1) (**Free Ebook**)
https://books2read.com/u/3yrBlV
His Mission (Book 2)
https://ellisoday.com/books/his-mission/
His Submission (Book 3)
https://ellisoday.com/books/his-submission/

LA PETITE MORT CLUB INTIMATE ENCOUNTER SERIES
YOU KNOW THE PLAYERS, BUT DO YOU KNOW THE KINK?

HIS LESSON (TERRY AND MAGGIE)
https://ellisoday.com/books/his-lesson/

PLAYING HOUSE (NICK AND SARAH)
https://ellisoday.com/books/playing-house

HIS LOVE (TERRY AND MAGGIE)
https://ellisoday.com/books/his-love/

HIS IMPERFECT DAY (TERRY AND MAGGIE)
https://ellisoday.com/books/his-imperfect-day

COMING SOON:

ETHAN'S STORY

HARKER and ALISON'S STORY

MATTIE'S STORY

JAKE'S STORY

REBECCA AND DEREK'S STORY

VIC'S STORY

Email me with questions, concerns or to let me know what you thought of the book. I love hearing from readers.
authorEllisOday@gmail.com

https://www.EllisODay.com

Follow me

Facebook
https://www.facebook.com/EllisODayRomanceAuthor/

Closed FB Group (sneak peeks, sample chapters, and other bonuses)

Ellis O. Day

https://www.facebook.com/groups/153238782143373

Bookbub
https://www.bookbub.com/authors/Ellis-o-day

Instagram
https://www.instagram.com/authorEllisOday/

Twitter
https://twitter.com/Ellis_o_day

Pinterest
www.pinterest.com\AuthorEllisODay

ABOUT THE AUTHOR

Ellis O. Day loves reading and writing about love and sex. She believes that although the two don't have to go together, it's best when they do (both in life and in fantasy).

Ellis O. Day

www.ingramcontent.com/pod-product-compliance
Lightning Source LLC
Chambersburg PA
CBHW030314180626
46810CB00003B/1068